Praise for *Cannibals:*
Stories from the Edge of the Pine Barrens

"Jen Conley has the rare ability to imbue her stories with an emotional heft that is both subtle and powerful within the darkness. Amongst the other writers with that similar skill set, none do it as well as she does."
—Todd Robinson, author of *The Hard Bounce*

"Far from the concrete wasteland of the Turnpike lies the dark heart of the Garden State, and *Cannibals* carves it out still beating. Jen Conley writes with the soul and poetry of Springsteen, pure blue collar Jersey Gothic. These stories take a big bite out of you."
—Thomas Pluck, author of *Blade of Dishonor*

"Few writers capture the meaning of what it means to be imprisoned better than Jen Conley."
—Joe Clifford, author of
Lamentation and *December Boys*

"Jen Conley builds her stories from both the minutiae and the grandeur of everyday life. The world in *Cannibals* is mostly a hardscrabble one, and it is the lucidity of her prose and the specificity of her settings and characters that make her one of the finest practitioners of the short story in crime fiction. This is an exciting, scary, compelling collection."
—Patricia Abbott, author of
Concrete Angel and *Shot in Detroit*

"Every time I start a new short by Jen Conley, I know I'm in for a treat. Her stories are so good that, even after they hit you in the gut and leave a bruise, you're thankful for it—so an entire collection is a real gift."
—Rob Hart, author of
New Yorked and *City of Rose*

D0220766

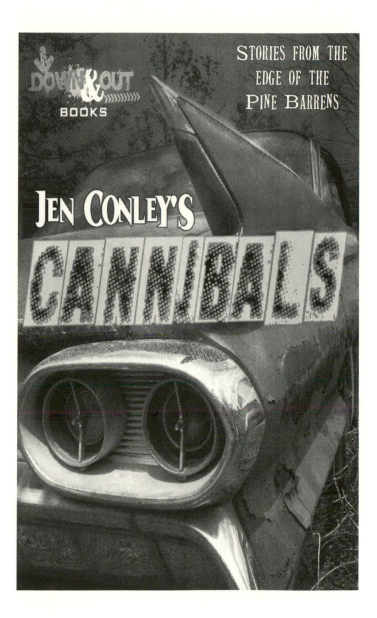

STORIES FROM THE
EDGE OF THE
PINE BARRENS

DOWN & OUT
BOOKS

JEN CONLEY'S

CANNIBALS

CANNIBALS

STORIES FROM THE EDGE OF THE PINE BARRENS

JEN CONLEY

Down & Out Books
3959 Van Dyke Rd, Ste. 265
Lutz, FL 33558
www.DownAndOutBooks.com

Cover design by James R. Tuck

ISBN: 1-943402-23-X
ISBN-13: 978-1-943402-23-6

CONTENTS

HOME INVASION

It was a cold winter night in 2001 when Keon Dell did his very first and only burglary. He had robbed before—held up a store by gunpoint (no bullets in that gun)—but he'd never broken into a house, much less a house owned by people who could afford a cleaning woman.

Just nineteen, the boy was tense and uneasy as he sat in the backseat of the dark sedan while Ramone—one of those roughened-up white guys who had done hard time—was in the passenger seat, giving directions to James, the one doing the driving. James and Keon were from the same neighborhood, but didn't know each other well. The guy steered the car with his left hand, his grip loose and relaxed, like they were heading out for pizza instead of a break-in.

Ramone wasn't referring to their plan as a break-in or a burglary. He referred to it as a *home invasion*, mocking the term used in newspapers these days. James had done a handful of them, he said, a couple of years back, and there was nothing to it. But this one wasn't James's idea—it was Ramone's baby. Ramone had a girl who lived out here, on the border of Burlington and Ocean counties. She knew about the house because she had been the cleaning woman; around here it was mostly woods and lonely back roads where the Jersey Devil was rumored to roam.

James smoked while he steered the car along the twisting and turning roads. In between giving directions, Ramone told the story about the Jersey Devil: how after Mrs. Leeds found out she was pregnant, she cursed the child because it was her thirteenth; how after it was born, it grew into a devil with horns, hooves, and bat wings, and then it beat everyone in the room bloody with its forked tail; how after the gory thrashing, it screeched a horrific cry and flew up the chimney.

James was originally from South Carolina, so he had never heard the story before, but Keon knew it well. He had been brought up in New Jersey and it was something all kids learned in school. "It's just culture. New Jersey culture," Keon remembered his fourth-grade teacher saying. But the story had scared him enough to press her about it. "Will the Jersey Devil come to my house?"

His teacher shook her head. She had thick brown freckles on her nose and cheeks. "No. He only bothers the people in south Jersey, in the Pine Barrens. We live in *central* Jersey."

Still, the story frightened little Keon and gave him nightmares.

Keon wasn't so little anymore—standing almost five-eleven. He was lean but muscular, not bad looking in a wiry sort of way. He was also the only one in the car who hadn't done time, although that was stupid-ass luck. Recently, he and TJ Jones had robbed an Indian man by gunpoint. Keon just walked right into the convenience store, put the gun to his head, and demanded the old man open the cash register. TJ grabbed the cash. "Thanks for following directions," Keon said to the man before they fled. And they were never caught.

"Right here, right here," Ramone said now. "Yeah. This is it." James turned the car onto the gravel road, a long driveway winding through thick woods until it ended at a large house. James flipped the lights off and Keon sucked in his breath, fingering the gun in his pocket. (This time, it was loaded.) Earlier, Ramone had explained that the owners of the house were in Ft. Lauderdale for the winter. Ramone's girl, who had been the cleaning woman for only a few months, had told him this. She was from Russia and very beautiful—naturally blonde and slim. She had an exotic face with Siamese eyes and wide-set cheekbones. "It's called the Slavic look," Ramone explained to Keon. "If I had it in me, I'd send her down to A.C. so she could make some serious cash in a club. But the thought of Olya sitting on some fat old shit for a lap dance makes me very ill."

Keon and Ramone worked together in the kitchen of a restaurant owned by a large man. Every few days, the man strutted into the kitchen, his huge chest and stomach protruding like the breast of a pigeon. "Make me a cheesesteak, Ramone. And don't put too many onions on it." His name was Dennis Cork. Ramone called him Dennis Pork.

What surprised Ramone was that Dennis had allowed Keon to work for him. "Dennis Pork don't hire brothers. He says they all steal. How'd you get yourself hired? He must have been hard up."

"Don't know," Keon said with a shrug. He had quit school in October after a fight with his Phys. Ed. teacher. "Go fuck yourself!" he had yelled. An hour later, the school secretary explained he had earned himself three days' suspension. "Fuck off," he told her and the next day quit. It didn't matter much anyway. He was supposed to be a senior but he only had enough credits to be a sophomore. Not long afterwards, Keon got a job at Dennis Cork's restaurant.

Ramone agreed with his decision. "Just get your GED. You ain't heading for college, are ya, Colin Powell?" Ramone had his GED, something he got while he was doing time. Ramone had a ten-inch scar that started on the left side of his neck and traveled down his chest in a jagged angle. His arms were covered in black tattoos. He had spent his teen years in Jamesburg—a rough juvie for boys— and a couple more years up in Rahway State Prison. He was missing his right pinkie finger. After working besides each other for some time, Ramone explained how he had come to lose it. "When I was a kid, my mother ran with this motherfucker for a while. One afternoon, he was drinking hard and he got mad at me when I dropped the milk all over the kitchen floor. So he grabbed me, took something like this," Ramone held up the cleaver he was using to cut a piece of raw beef into strips, "and held my hand on the counter and chopped it off like this." Ramone placed the cleaver over the meat, rocked it forward and backwards, slicing through the pinkish beef. Then he lifted the piece up and let it dangle from his hand. "My finger came off just like that. Quick and clean, brother."

Keon stared at the pink strip of meat. "How old were you?"

Ramone shrugged. "Eight."

Keon nodded like it was nothing, but he shuddered inside. He himself had been in and out of foster homes and now lived with his grandmother in a dilapidated neighborhood. He had seen his share of shit, but for some reason like the story of the Jersey Devil, the missing pinkie story gnawed at him like a mad ringing in the ear.

"Olya says there's a key in a flower pot," Ramone said after James killed the engine. "Next to the back door."

A lamp glowed in the front window of the house. James chuckled and said it was probably one of those keep-robbers-away lights. "Make people like us think they're home." He lit a cigarette. "And then we'd stay away."

Olya had worked for these people for five months until the woman had let her go. There was nothing she did wrong, the woman told Olya; her husband simply wanted to cut back on expenses. Olya said fine, finished up her work, and left pleasantly. There was no bad blood. Yet there were some things Olya observed or learned that she eventually spilled to Ramone: the woman had a lot of jewelry; the husband kept a box of cash in his desk drawer; apparently, they went to Florida every year after Christmas and stayed until Mother's Day.

"They're stupid people, leaving keys around," Ramone said. "Dumb-asses."

"Let's go," James said.

They got out of the car and headed towards the back. The night was cold and Keon shivered as he walked along the gravel driveway. His stomach was in knots—he was real nervous—talking about the Jersey Devil had given him a bad premonition.

The moon, full and bright, revealed a clear view of the large house, which had two floors, a porch that wrapped around the side, and low long windows. In the backyard, a shiny black iron fence enclosing a covered in-ground pool, glimmered softly in the white moonlight. Thick woods sur-rounded the property, keeping it nestled and cozy, like something in a fairy tale.

The three of them put on gloves.

The key was indeed in an empty pot near the door. Keon shook his head—he was bothered by this stupidity. Ramone grinned. "Olya says they have a daughter who comes and checks on the house once a week."

"Then why don't they just give her a key?"

He opened the door. "I know, brother. Stupid people. Dumb-asses."

James stood outside and smoked. Keon, shivering from the cold (and from nerves,) stared at him. "What're you doing? Smoke inside. It's freezing out here."

James took one more drag and then dropped it on the ground. "Habit, man. My mom makes me smoke outside." Keon nodded and held the door for James to pass through.

They entered into the kitchen, which was the largest indoor kitchen Keon had ever seen. The counters were bare and they gleamed, even in the slight darkness. A dishtowel hung along the counter in front of the sink. The kitchen connected to the living room, where a lamp shone near the front window. Ramone and James walked around, poking their heads behind the plaid couches, picking up wooden knickknacks, flipping through old magazines that sat on the tables. Keon sighed impatiently. He peered out one of the kitchen windows and walked into the living room. He was nauseous now. "Can we get this done?"

Ramone turned to him. "You okay, brother?"

Keon shrugged, trying to play it cool. "I just want to get this done."

Ramone told him to go upstairs and find the jewelry. He and James would look for the cash. Keon nodded and climbed the carpeted staircase. He held a small flashlight and flipped it on when he reached the upstairs hallway, guessing the master bedroom was the last door on the left. When he arrived, he pushed the door open and, to his horror, immediately saw the bed was rumpled and unmade. Keon stood for a second and listened, swinging the flashlight about the room, over the bed and dressers. An overturned open book lay on the night table. Worn jeans, a thick red sweater, and a large white bra were draped on the far chair. His heart knocked hard in his chest. He pulled his left glove off and placed his hand on the white sheet—a trick he had seen in a movie. The mattress was warm.

When Keon had stuck the gun against the Indian man's head, there was a sense that he was playing, like when he was a little kid and imagined he was a bank robber. He knew the man would be scared and do what he said. He knew nothing was going to go wrong. Hell, there were no bullets. And because it happened so fast—like that freefall amusement ride at the Boardwalk—he had no time for a nervous stomach.

But now, this was different. This whole thing

was taking too long—the drive out to the house, that Ramone and James were taking a leisurely approach—everything seemed bizarre and doomed. Keon inhaled deeply and then exhaled. He swung the flashlight back to the night table and looked at the telephone. She'd called the police, hadn't she? He tugged the glove back on and picked up the old white phone.

There was no dial tone. It didn't work.

He put it down and listened again. He could hear James and Ramone downstairs, moving around, banging things around, their voices muffled.

A small movement came from the closet. Keon froze. He decided not to check it yet. He did nothing but feel the gun in his pocket.

And then Ramone appeared. He swung his flashlight across the room until he found Keon. Instantly, Ramone noticed something was off. Keon swallowed and nodded, pretending he had everything under control. Ramone pointed to the closet door and, after hesitating for a moment, Keon nodded once more.

Ramone smirked and pointed. *Check it out.*

Keon took a deep breath and waited, but Ramone's eyes were on him. Keon's hands shook.

"Boy!" Ramone hissed.

Keon pulled out his gun, walked to the closet, and opened the door. He shone the flashlight and there she was, huddled in the corner, under the

9

hanging clothes. She let out a timid yet frenzied cry.

"Get up," Keon ordered. It took a long minute, but she wrenched herself out from the corner and stood, whimpering. She was a woman in her sixties, bland in the face with coarse dark hair. She wore a flannel red nightgown and white puffy socks. She looked familiar to him.

Ramone stuck his head into the closet and pointed his gun towards the woman. "Looky-here!"

The woman wept.

"The phone's dead—I checked it," Keon said quickly. "So no police were called."

Ramone lowered the gun and turned to Keon. "Young man, you make me proud!" His voice sizzled like burning eggs on a skillet.

Keon said nothing.

Ramone ordered the woman to step out of the closet, and he and Keon moved aside as she stumbled forward, trembling and muttering, the flashlight making shadows bounce from ceiling to floor to the woman. Keon caught quick glimpses of her face. Yes, she resembled someone he knew.

"This ain't good," Ramone remarked, clucking his tongue. "No good at all." Then, suddenly and oddly, Ramone announced he had to check on James—he didn't trust the dickhead, you see. "We've had issues."

"Can you handle this?" Ramone asked.

"Yeah," Keon said.

Ramone, seeming satisfied, walked away. But before he left, he flipped on the overhead lamp. "No point using flashlights if the lady of the house is home, is there?"

Instantly, in the new harsh light, Keon recognized her: Mrs. Mullins, his seventh grade math teacher. He'd only had her for a few months because he wasn't at that school for long. Eventually he was removed from the foster home he was living in and sent back to his grandmother's.

She didn't let on that she recognized him, which was good. Keon pointed his gun, directing her to walk to the bed and sit on it. She did so obediently.

Keon asked where she kept the jewelry.

She pointed to the top drawer of her dresser. "There's a lot in there," she said, her voice quivering, reminding Kean of the way his grandmother's tea cups slightly rattled in the cheap china cabinet. "You can get plenty for them."

Keon shoved the gun in the back pocket of his jeans. "You got no safe?"

"It's in the basement," she whispered.

Again, Ramone appeared in the doorway and he grinned widely. "In the basement? So there's more money than what's in the desk drawer?"

Mrs. Mullins peered up at Ramone and then dropped her head. He glared at her for a long moment before he spoke once more: "Lady, your age and ugliness is gonna save you from you-know-what."

She looked up, terrified.

Keon felt a nasty chill ride through him.

Ramone chuckled. "I'm going downstairs again. I'll be back in a second."

Keon turned to the dresser drawer, picking up rings and necklaces. "Is this real?" he asked, holding up a piece. "Don't give me any shit. If I find out any of this is fake, I'll come back."

"I know you," she finally said, her voice rattling now. "You're Keon. Keon Dell."

Keon paused for a second, his breath halting short, his heart thrashing against his ribs like a thick, mean hammer. He forced himself to carry on and shuffled through the drawer. "That ain't my name."

"Yes. I was a teacher and I had you a few years ago, right before I retired. I remember all my troubled students."

Keon picked up a thick, gold bangle. His hand shook. "This real?"

She nodded. "You lived with that nice family, the Lauber's." Her voice acquired a hopeful tone. "They still take in kids, you know."

Once again, Keon told her she was mistaken. She hadn't been a teacher he particularly liked. She was nasty, screaming at kids who daydreamed or had no explanation why they were missing homework. She had yelled at him, too, for slouching at his desk, his newly grown long limbs stretched out into the aisle and his hands stuffed in his pants pockets.

"Pay attention, Mr. Dell! Or you'll be paying attention tomorrow afternoon in detention."

Keon liked that school, though. Mostly it was white kids, but there were a handful of black and Hispanic students. He was popular, being all street and tough. He had been living with the Lauber's since the beginning of sixth grade, and by the time the summer began, he had grown to love his clean bed and the steadiness of the family. Every Thursday, Mrs. Lauber let him choose the dinner menu. Most times, he picked tacos or her home-made mac and cheese with hotdogs. In seventh grade, he made the basketball team, but he only played four games, because after Christmas the state sent him back to his grandmother's. "You gonna behave this time," she told him. But he had never behaved for her, no matter what she said. "When your mother gets back, she's gonna be horrified at how you conduct yourself." He hadn't seen his mother since he was ten, hadn't lived with her since he was six. She was up in Brooklyn somewhere, with some man.

He didn't stay with his grandmother for long after the Lauber's. He was sent to a group home for a while, and then another foster home, and another, and then back with his grandmother. All told, by the time he had turned eighteen, he had been in five different homes. Yet the Lauber's had been the best. Still to this day, Keon pulled out the recipe for that mac and cheese with the hotdogs and made it for himself and his grandmother. "Not bad," she'd always say. "Not bad at all."

"You must remember me," Mrs. Mullins said. "I yelled at you all the time."

Keon shook his head. "Nope." He had a sack for the jewelry and when he was satisfied he had taken all the valuable stuff, he closed the drawer. "What about your husband? Does he have something? A watch maybe?"

She said no.

"Where is he, anyway?"

"Florida."

Keon became angry. This was a stupid lady. The phone was off. The key was in a flower pot. She didn't even try to lie and say her husband would be home any minute. "Now why tell me your husband ain't nowhere near this place? Why not tell me he's on his way home?"

She shrugged. "You do remember me, Keon? I gave you detention a few times and you always came."

Ramone stood in the doorway. "She knows you?"

You stupid woman, Keon thought, his heart sinking.

Ramone walk forward, pulled out his gun, and put it to her head. "You know him?"

She shook violently, but controlled her voice, even taking on a slight authoritative tone—surely an old defensive strategy from her teaching days.

"Yes. Keon was a student of mine."

Ramone laughed. "Now how fucked up is that?" He moved the gun away and shoved it in his back pocket. He picked up a pillow and tossed it to Keon. "They have a basement. The mister has it all decked out like an English pub, but there ain't no beer on tap. Imagine that?" He flicked his head towards the woman. "Let her give you a tour. Let her open the safe for you." He eyeballed her. "You know the combination, right?"

She said she did.

Ramone glared at Keon. "It's right behind the bar."

Keon shook his head. "Get James to do it."

"He's busy. Get going." Ramone pulled the woman up and pushed her to the door. He grabbed the sack from Keon. "Go on, boy."

They walked downstairs and passed James, who leaned against a wall in the kitchen. He nodded, opened the basement door, leaned in, and held out his hand like a game show host. "Check it out, man. It's cool."

The steps were wooden and they creaked as Keon and Mrs. Mullins made their way down. With his right hand he held his gun and pointed it at her back, and with his left hand, he gripped the pillow, his stomach sick with anxiety. The basement was large, carpeted, and paneled in dark brown. A mahogany bar sat in the far corner with a dozen or so bottles hanging upside down. There

15

were three taps and bar towels and thick ashtrays—all with names of beers Keon didn't recognize. He looked around, searching for a way out. To the far left, he noticed a glass door. "Where does that go?" he asked her.

"To stairs that lead outside to the pool. I had Alan put it in for the grandkids. This way they can take their wet clothes off without getting water all over my house." Her voice was rickety and frightened, yet she pressed on, annoying Keon. "I have five grandchildren. I love them to death. You should see my Visa bill at Christmastime." Her tormented chatter *knock-knock-knocked* in his head. He needed to think and her talking distracted him.

"Keon, do you have any sisters or brothers?" she asked. "I adored my brother. Oh, how I worshiped him. Do you have any siblings?"

Keon didn't answer. He walked backwards, holding the gun so it faced her, and tried the door. It was bolted. He walked towards her again. He was shaking now. "Why's the phone off?"

She swallowed. "Because I'm usually in Florida. We turn that and the cable off to save money. I'm just here for a few days. My friend died. You might remember her. Mrs. Lattori? She taught math."

He vaguely recalled a tall, skinny woman with short, black hair.

"She walked with a cane. I'm sure she had the cane when you were there." He now clearly saw the woman limping in the hall, a three-pronged gray metal cane at her side. "MS," Mrs. Mullins said. "Multiple Sclerosis."

"What's in the safe? More jewelry?"

"Cash. Money. Our passports. Birth certificates."

Keon let out a disgusted deep breath. He never understood why regular people kept cash in the house. "Why does your husband leave money in the house? Why not leave it in the bank?"

She trembled. "Emergency." Her voice quivered. "We leave it when we go to Florida for our daughter in case she needs it. He's old fashioned. He thinks people should always have cash on them." She continued talking and shaking. "A lot of us older people keep cash at home. They don't trust the banks. I guess Alan has some of that in him. The safe is fire-proof, too."

He still didn't understand. "Then why does he got money in the desk upstairs?"

Mrs. Mullins blinked her eyes and shrugged sadly.

Keon decided to move on. "You sure you know the combination to the safe?"

She nodded. "Yes."

"Good. Open it now."

They walked over to the bar and behind it, on the second shelf, sat a small beige safe. Mrs. Mullins bent down and, with trembling hands, twirled the dial three times until it opened. She pulled everything out—papers, passports, cash—and placed them on the counter. Keon could hear James and Ramone walking around upstairs, the front and back doors opening and closing. What were they doing? Keeping watch?

"That's all there is, I swear," she said.

He told her to come out from the bar and walk towards the glass door.

"Keon," Mrs. Mullins began.

"Shut up," he whispered. He looked at the glass door. He wanted her to hit him—no, to kick him, right in the groin, so he could double over and she could make a run for it. He still held the pillow in his hand.

He stared at the door once more. She didn't seem to catch on, so he decided he would have to tell her what to do.

But there was no time. Suddenly, Ramone came bounding down the stairs, laughing. "What're you doing, boy?"

Keon didn't answer. Ramone shook his head, annoyed. "Give me this." He grabbed the pillow from Keon, put it against Mrs. Mullins head, and with his other hand, pulled out his gun, sticking it against the pillow. She screamed and shook horrendously, but she did not try to get away. She only pleaded for her life, her voice desperate, her pitch high and frantic: *"No! No, please! Don't! I love my grandchildren!"*

Ramone tilted his head and gazed at Keon. Keon

opened his mouth to—do what—stop the motion? But Ramone returned his focus to the task before him and, simply, fired.

Her body buckled and collapsed. White stuffing dotted with red floated in the air. Ramone threw the pillow next to the body. Blood and pieces of gray seeped out of her head and onto the floor, a greenish carpet with swirling gold designs. Keon and Ramone stared at the body. "She said she taught you math?"

Keon nodded. He was stunned and sickened and it took everything in him not to cry out. "Yeah," he muttered.

Ramone slipped his gun in his pocket. He walked behind the bar, grabbed the cash and several bottles of scotch. "Help me and let's go."

They shut the back door when they left. James bent down to the ground and picked up the cigarette he had smoked before. "Don't want them getting my DNA now."

James drove the car in reverse down the long gravel driveway. Keon watched the light in the front window disappear as it became blocked by trees, his heart so horribly sickened, he imagined it was gray and shriveled—contaminated.

They split the five thousand in cash and each of them took some jewelry and scotch. Keon got a few gold necklaces and a diamond ring. Too young to have acquired a taste for scotch, he gave his two bottles to old Mr. Cooper next door.

Keon read his grandmother's newspaper every day as they followed the murder of Barbara Mullins, age sixty-three, mother of two, grandmother of five. Nothing was ever traced back to them, not even to Olya. "She paid me off the books," Olya said one night, a few weeks later, while they all hung out. "And she always call me Tatiana. So I just answer to that." Whether Olya knew the details of what happened that night, Ramone never said.

By summertime, Olya and Ramone had moved to California. She wanted to live in San Diego and Ramone said he liked the idea of her wearing a bikini twelve months out of the year. As for James, he got into some hot water with someone from the neighborhood and had to slip out of town.

On a humid July afternoon, Keon walked by an Army recruiting station. He stopped and stood before the glass windows, staring at the posters of young men and women in their military uniforms, gazing proudly into the blue sky. Keon went inside. Once he sat down, his hands stuffed in his pockets, the recruiter asked him if he liked the idea of seeing the world. "Europe, Japan, Hawaii."

Keon thought for a moment and then said, "I could be happy in Hawaii." The recruiter laughed.

Keon took his hands out of his pockets and sat up straight, suddenly reviewing his life. He had nothing now. The diamond ring he got from the robbery was cracked and the gold bangles weren't worth much. There wasn't much cash left after a couple of months. He was sleeping on Old Mr. Cooper's couch because his grandmother had kicked him out a week earlier, after had she found fifty dollars missing. Keon hadn't taken it, but she didn't believe him. He didn't have a good behavioral record to back it up.

So he joined the Army. And after a few months, 9/11 happened. And after that, Iraq was invaded. He never saw Japan or Hawaii. However, it wasn't all bad. The good thing about being a soldier in a war, Keon thought, was that so many things got jumbled up. For the longest time, after Ramone shot Mrs. Mullins, Keon woke in the middle of the night, like he did when he was a kid, dreaming of the Jersey Devil. Yet, it wasn't just the Jersey Devil he was dreaming of now. He was dreaming of Ramone's finger, and Mrs. Mullins and her blood and brains. But now that he was a combat soldier, the blood and brains of his kills got all mixed with Mrs. Mullins and Ramone's finger and sometimes, on a good night, all that evil confused him. And for a brief moment, when he was sitting up, wide awake, breathing hard, getting his bearings, the last traces of the dream breaking up and dissolving, it was like he was a kid again telling himself that the

Jersey Devil was just a story. For a brief moment, after waking from the dream, mercy would fall upon him, and he would tell himself Mrs. Mullins and her bloody death never actually happened.

Previously published in Thuglit.

CANNIBALS

The girl was a tomboy and she could handle herself in the woods without her stupid cousin and his idiot friend.

"There's cannibals back there," the cousin said.

"My uncle seen them," the friend added. Both boys snickered.

The girl, named Jade, didn't believe them. All three kids were at a standstill, scuffing their feet against the grayish-colored dirt trail, arguing which way to go. They weren't lost. They knew the way out of the woods but the boys thought they should go west and Jade thought they should go south. She said if they went her way, there'd be a ShopRite not far and she was hungry. The supermarket had a café and she hoped to get a sandwich. But her cousin insisted there was a pizza parlor his way and Jade said that she'd eaten there before and it was crap. In the end, the boys went west and she went south. Before they parted, the boys warned her once again about the cannibals in the woods.

"Shut up," Jade snapped.

The boys turned, shaking their heads and laughing.

"Do you like leg or arm?" the idiot friend called

to the cousin and the cousin replied, "Only with barbeque sauce." Those were the last words Jade heard from them.

She began walking, tromping through the trail, which grew narrower as she went and more covered with dead leaves and pine needles that cracked underneath her footfalls. The trail twisted through the forest, going up a little hill and then down, but mostly it was flat land. Jade could hear the soft whirr of the Parkway in the distance. The air had an icy dry bite to it and the pale winter sun glimmered through the scrub pines and white oaks weakly because it was late, around four o'clock. Jade pretended she was on an adventure, with fantastical creatures from far-off lands hiding in the trees, and she imagined they had their own language which only she could understand. At twelve, she was dreamy at times, drifting into her own world, an escape from everyone else. But she could leave her fantasy world in an instant and return to reality, especially if there was trouble brewing and she had to defend herself. True, Jade had a small frame and was skinny as a twig, but she was whip fast, as anyone watching her on the soccer field could tell, and she could still take a punch from her brothers and cousins and their friends. Jade had a quarter-inch scar at the side of her left eye because last year a rusted bicycle chain flew out of her brother's hand and slapped into her face by mistake.

She was thinking about the creatures when she came upon the men.

There was a small clearing and a strange small building made of stone and the men's camp was only about ten feet from the building. The building was no bigger than a shed and it was graffitied and the wooden door had an iron-cast gate over it. There were three men and they sat by their scruffy tents in front of a small campfire. They did not stand or say a word to Jade but they watched her with dark black eyes, their faces sunken in, like collapsed roofs. She stopped for a moment, not sure whether to turn and go back the way she came, or to continue on because the ShopRite was just past the clearing, down the hill. She knew this for sure. And by the way the men looked at her, instinctively she knew whichever way she chose, she would have to run.

So, like a freaked-out rabbit, she took off, rushing past the stone shed, past the men's camp, belting with speed like she were going for a goal. She didn't get far. The third man leapt up and jumped in her path, snatching her by the waist and swinging her around to face him.

"Hahaha," he croaked, seizing her little wrist and pulling her towards him.

"Let me go!" she cried, struggling to break free.

"Nah," he said, laughing. Jade squirmed and jerked, but he got a good hold of her by gripping both of her upper arms with strong hands. His laugh halted. "Stop your moving, girly," he growled and Jade listened.

"Where you going?" he demanded. His mouth was large and full of broken, yellow teeth and hair was stringy and thin, long, pulled into a pony tail. He reeked of foul smells like piss and whiskey and unwashed skin. "Huh?"

Jade said nothing. The stench from his mouth was ghastly.

"Where you going?"

The girl forced herself to stay collected, not cry. "I'm going to ShopRite."

"What's in ShopRite?"

"I'm hungry."

"So you have money on you?"

He wanted her money. She was about to be robbed.

"How much money do you have on you?"

Jade swallowed. "Like four dollars and twenty-five cents." This was true.

"Four dollars and twenty-five cents," he repeated, mimicking her voice. His hands clutched her arms and he squeezed. She tried not to show pain or fear.

"What are you gonna buy with four dollars and twenty-five cents?"

"I don't know," Jade said, trembling. "Food."

"Yeah, I know that. What kind a food?"

"A sandwich."

"Mmmm," the man said with a lusty sound in

his voice, his breath close and hideous. "I could go for a sandwich. A nice, moist ham sandwich with Swiss cheese."

"I gotta go," Jade said suddenly. Then a lie came from her mouth: "My cousin and his friend are waiting for me."

"At ShopRite?"

"Yeah."

The man still held her upper arms like the claws of some monster as if he sensed she might take off. "They're waiting for you?"

"Yeah."

The man let his hands relax and Jade attempted to shake free, but he was quick and seized her by the wrist. "I'm hungry too," he whispered and it made the girl shudder so deep, her young bones seemed to rattle. They were cannibals.

"Let's go for a walk, sweetie," the man said.

"I don't want to."

"I got something to show you," he said and pulled her along. They walked through the brush and Jade heard crows call. She knew they traveled in something called a *murder* and they watched out for each other. She wanted them to watch out for her now.

The man led her to the strange building, his hand clenched around her tiny forearm like a handcuff. "You know what's in there?"

"No."

"A well."

Tears began to form in Jade's eyes. He was going to drown her.

"Years ago," the man said quietly, "back in the settlement times, the early seventeen hundreds, there used to be a little town in this clearing and they had a witch in the town. She wasn't a terrible witch but she got angry at the townspeople because they didn't let her come to their social gatherings and they made her move out to a tiny house in the woods. So she cast a spell and sent smallpox to the people. Many of them died. Those that lived knew it was the witch's fault, so they threw her in the well."

The grasp on her arm got tighter.

"You gotta understand, girly," the man said, "that long ago, there wasn't no shed."

Jade nodded, but kept her eyes on the cast iron gate.

"Yeah, so they tossed her in the well and because she was a witch, she lasted longer than the average person. She screamed and scratched her hands against the walls until they were bloody. The witch cursed the people before she finally slipped away under the water."

Jade tried to move away but his grip got tighter.

"But that ain't it. For years and years, late at night, the townspeople would hear her cries and curses—she was haunting them. So they built this stone shed over the well to stop the noise but it didn't work. The people could still hear it so they moved away and left nothing but this clearing."

Abruptly, the man pushed Jade against the gated door. "If you put your ear against the wall, you can hear the witch's voice."

Jade moved her head so her ear was against the wall. She heard nothing. "Must only happen at night," she said nervously.

The man smiled. "Yeah."

Jade removed her head from the gate and looked at the man. "I have to go now."

"No, you sit with us for a while."

Tears slipped out of her eyes. "I want to go."

"Not yet. I'm hungry too, so you'll suffer with us. See what if feels like."

Jade looked at the man with the sunken face and large mouth and dark eyes. One of the other men from the camp stood and made his way over to the girl.

"She got some money in her pockets," the man with the large mouth stated to the second man, his voice changing from menacing to something stiff and cold.

While the first man held her arms, the second man patted the girl down, like they did in police television shows. He ran both hands up her legs, around her waist, her arms, then he checked her pockets and found her purple change purse. "Cool," the second man said, taking the purse and walking back to the camp.

The man with the large mouth stared at Jade for

a long awkward moment, her forearm still in his firm grip. Finally he said, "You gonna be a beautiful woman in a couple of years. A little makeup, lipstick, you gonna have all the boys after you. Even with that little ugly scar near your eyeball."

Jade turned her head away from him and looked into the woods. The fear in her soul was deep.

Suddenly the man jerked his head up and said, "Ah, I hear it. Listen."

Jade listened but heard nothing.

"The witch. She's calling. Come on." He shoved her closer to the building. The stench of him was appalling. Like a broken septic tank.

"Hear it?" he asked.

Jade didn't.

"Oooooo," the man crooned. "She's calling to us."

Nothing.

He gazed at Jade. "You hear it, sweetie?"

"No," she said. "I'm sorry."

He seemed to grow angry. "You ain't listening hard enough." He took his free hand and, oddly, almost gently pressed her head against the wall. "You'll hear it now."

Jade swallowed and closed her eyes and tried to hear the witch, but there was still nothing. She decided this time, though, she would claim she did hear her cries. Perhaps that would make him let go of her arm. "Wait, yeah, I hear it," she said.

The man squinted his eyes and hissed, "You're a liar." The two were so close, she feared he might kiss her.

"Liar," he whispered.

"No, I'm not. I did hear it."

"You're lying."

She didn't know what to say. She looked at him and then away at the camp, where the other two men sat, and then towards the opening to the trail across the clearing which would lead her to ShopRite. "Can I go now?" Jade whined, leaning away from him. "Please. My cousin and his friend—"

"Your cousin and that friend ain't nowhere with you now. They went a different way."

Jade shook her head. "Yeah, but they'll be there waiting for me at ShopRite. We're playing a game. Who can get there first."

"Liar," the man sneered, becoming furious. His grasp on her arm was so tight, if felt like he might snap it off her body. "No. They went the other way. They went for pizza."

Jade stared at the hideous man. How did he know this?

He licked his teeth, closed his large mouth, and then spit. From the corner of her eye, Jade saw the third man stand up. Something gleamed in that man's hand.

The first man, the man who held Jade, heard the third man behind him, and he turned to look. His grip loosened on her arm for a slight second and Jade twisted out of his hold and began to run. The murder of crows flew out of the trees as she heard footfalls behind her, but adrenaline made her even faster. She tore across the clearing, through the opening to the next trail, up a small mound and then down again, before she ran into another man, smashing into him and the box he held, knocking herself backwards.

"Whoa!" he said.

She staggered a bit, but reoriented herself as quickly as she could.

"Are you okay?" the guy said, placing the box down, which was full of cans and boxes of food. This man wore a bright green jacket and clean jeans. His head was bald. "Miss?"

"Yes," she said, getting ready to run again.

"Are you okay?" the guy asked.

She nodded. "Yes."

He stared at her suspiciously. "Did you meet Bowler and the other two men?"

Jade just looked at him.

His face grew angry. "Did they hurt you?" he demanded.

"I want to go home," she choked out.

"Did they hurt you? Where did they hurt you?" His voice was harsh and commanding, like a teacher's, so Jade pushed up her jacket sleeve and showed her forearm. Large ruddy marks smoldered on her pale skin.

"Which one did that?"

She didn't know how to describe the man with the large mouth and yellow teeth, so she shrugged.

The guy in the bright green jacket shook his head in disgust. Still, Jade didn't trust him. She pushed down her sleeve and like a buckshot, took off running, racing down the hill, through the dusty trail, her brain saying, *Go go go.*

She ran until she smelled fire again and suddenly found herself in another camp, this one bigger and more populated. Jade stopped and stood, her heart broken with fear. She glanced around, searching for the best escape route through the camp. Some of the people looked at her and a woman with crazy hair appeared from nowhere, chattering. "You lost, honey? You lost?" Jade jumped back. Abruptly, she wheeled around and took off again, scampering through the array of tents, shacks, and even a couple of broken down cars, not sure if this was the right direction but her gut said it was. Nobody said anything to her as she ran and within a minute she made it to the blacktop, the far corner of the ShopRite parking lot. It was empty where she came out and because she was afraid one of the people from the tents might come get her, she continued to run, sprinting across the black tar, through the vehicles until she got to the doors of the supermarket, and only then did she turn around to look if she was being followed. No one. She stared across the parking lot. The sun had gone down and the last wisps of orange and yellow light glowed over the tree tops.

Inside, she found a payphone and called her oldest brother with a quarter she found in her pocket—something the one man who had patted her down hadn't found. Her brother promised to come get her in fifteen minutes. Jade watched for him from inside the store, looking through a dirty window.

While she waited with her hands shoved in her jacket pockets, she tried to force herself not to think about the witch in the well and the cannibals she had met, but it was futile. The men's horrid faces and the witch's story and the smell of man with the large mouth punched around her mind like flies against glass. She wondered why the men didn't live in the other camp with the others. Then she realized they had been kicked out of the regular camp because they were cannibals.

Or something else.

Her brother soon arrived. She told him nothing.

Previously published in Beat to a Pulp.

HOWLING

I walk along the side of the small house, my flashlight steady, the last of dark summer night hanging over me, when a rustle occurs and something hard blasts into my upper right arm. It takes a second, a delay, but the hit does the job—sheer fucking pain.

"Goddammit!" I yell, bending forward, gritting through the throbbing ache. I'm a forty-five year-old female police officer, on the force eighteen years, and bone tired of dealing with the crazed elderly.

Ralph Palczynski, ninety-plus, stands before me with a baseball bat. The hit hasn't broken anything but obviously the man can still manage a piss-mean swing.

"Ralph, what the hell are you doing?" I grunt, shining the flashlight in his face.

"Uh-oh," Ralph Palczynski mutters. "I'm sorry, miss, Officer Vogel."

"Jesus Christ."

"Please, I'm sorry."

I grit my teeth. This is my own friggin' fault—I should have knocked on the man's door before going around the side of his house. It's just that when I got out of the car, I thought I heard something strange, like a hollow whine, a weird cry. But after a quick investigation, I saw it was a cat prowling along the edge of the backyard and woods. Ralph caught me on the return from the strange-noise hunt.

"Can we stand somewhere else, Mr. Palczynski?" I ask, shining my flashlight on him. "Like on your front porch?"

"I told you to call me Ralph, Officer. And you're welcome to come inside my house."

I flash the light towards the ground with my left hand and roll my right shoulder in attempt to kick out the lingering pain. There's gonna be a bruise on my upper arm—something Carl, who was killed in a car wreck two months ago, would have been angry about. "It's not natural for women to do police work," he'd always said.

Mr. Palczynski turns and walks around the house. His gait is slow.

"It was you who called nine-one-one?" I say loudly, trailing behind him. "You knew I was coming, right?"

Ralph doesn't say anything for a moment. This is the third time he's called in the last three days. Ralph and I are familiar now, like bartender and regular.

"Yes, yes, of course," the old man finally replies when we reach the front of the house.

I shake my head and scan the retirement neighborhood. Streetlights are still shining. Living room lamps glow in the tiny houses all around—the presence of my patrol car no doubt waking people up. Across the street, an elderly couple steps out onto their porch. A man walks slowly down his driveway. A woman approaches from the house next door and stops.

"Everything's fine," I call out.

Nobody moves.

"Everything is fine, folks!"

Still, they don't move.

Inside, I stand in Ralph Palczynski's small powder-blue kitchen. He offers me whiskey but I turn him down. Despite the fact that I'm on duty and not much of a drinker, it is also four-thirty in the morning.

"I ain't crazy," Ralph begins. His hand shakes when he passes me a glass of water. "Those voices are still out there, Officer. The cries for help. A howling. Like something's being broiled alive." Ralph has an old-time New York accent. Queens, the Bronx, Archie Bunker. Someone who moved down to this south Jersey township after retirement. "Something's out there, Officer. Or it was, at least. Haven't heard it in a few hours."

Frustrated, I place the glass of water on the counter. "Right. And I told you last night I sent someone and he found nothing."

Ralph tilts his head. "Who'd you send? A rookie cop?"

A rookie cop. People watch too much TV. "Mr. Palczynski," I say, trying to remain patient. "We looked into it."

"Huh," the old man mutters, nodding, thinking. Then he says, "Maybe the cop didn't do the job, you know? Maybe he went to the bar. Maybe to see his broad on the side."

"Instead of checking out the voices?"

Ralph gazes at me. "Yes. That's the only explanation, ain't it?"

I close my eyes and then open them. "I suppose so."

"Officer," the old man says. "I told you I ain't gone crazy like half these people on this godforsaken reservation."

The old guy is a character. "Reservation?" I say.

"My wits are with me."

"I understand, Mr. Palczynski."

"Morning's coming. I think you should go out there yourself."

I did not want to go anywhere but home, yet I wanted to put an end to Ralph's I-hear-voices-in-the-back-woods shit. The morning before, after the second visit to Ralph's, I had asked dispatch to send one of the new guys to check out the fire trails behind the retirement development, and the reply was that nothing had been found.

"Is Vogel a German name?" Ralph suddenly asks.

I say yes. "Great-grandfather was from the

Munich area." I mean Carl's great-grandfather, but I don't explain it.

Ralph nods. "I spent some time in Germany. In World War II."

This piques my interest. I've lived all my life in this township, this desolate wooded place with a half-dozen retirement communities, and as a teenager, while I worked at McDonald's and then at the supermarket, I listened to the senior citizens tell me their life stories. I learned to tune out their tales unless they had something interesting to say about the Depression or the War. I've always enjoyed history, from any time period. I've read all of John McCulloughs's books, a couple biographies on Eleanor Roosevelt, Elizabeth I. I've traveled to England, France, and Machu Picchu. Most people like to go to the Islands, sit on the beach and stay good and drunk. Not me. Historical-themed travel is usually my preference.

But at the moment, I'm not into learning anything. I'm tired.

"So, Mr. Palczynski. Why don't we call this a night?"

The old man ignores my question and stares ominously into my eyes. "You ever seen a starved, dead person?"

If this is an idea of a dry joke, then it's not funny, because yes, I have. I've seen a lot over the years. Lonely elderly people who let themselves slip away by refusing food. Caregivers who starve their own parents.

"Very unsettling," Ralph says seriously. "War."

He obviously wants to talk. "Where was your tour in Germany?" I ask.

Ralph waves his hand at me. "I don't speak about it."

They always say they don't speak about it but they always do, and the old man is no different. "My poor wife. Bless her soul in heaven. She helped me with those nightmares about the war. They're something."

It takes me off guard, but sorrow suddenly overwhelms me. "When'd you lose your wife?"

"Last year. Married her in forty-six."

"Sounds like a good long run," I say, managing a gentle smile.

"Ah, marriage ain't no picnic," Ralph says, chuckling. "I wasn't always a stellar husband. Hollered too much. Strayed with one of the neighbors. A man can't resist a good pair of legs, can he?"

I fight the urge to roll my eyes. Fucking men. Even the old ones suck.

Ralph seems to go somewhere else for a moment, so I glance around the house, noticing the place is dusty. Women clean up the dust, don't they?

"Ah," the old guy mutters. "Wadda ya gonna do? Life. It'll kill ya."

I nod my head.

"So you gonna investigate?"

After asking a couple of Ralph's neighbors about the noises—one was deaf, another only thought they'd heard something—I make my way through the woods behind Ralph's house. I tromp over leaves and pine needles, the gray morning gray light quickly coming on, the air humid now, sweat dripping down my face. Sticker bushes stop me at one point and I stand motionless, glancing around, listening to a gentle breeze move the brush. The pine trees and oaks are bone dry—one spark could set the place up. I remember the fire of 1995. The damn flames jumped the Parkway. The smell of burnt wood and earth stank in my nostrils for weeks. Carl had complained. "Goddamn place. We need to move to North Carolina."

They called me right away, when Carl hit the truck. He lay in the Honda Accord until they got the Jaws of Life to pull him out. I held his hand, ignoring the ghoulish gashes in his face, blood soaking his shirt. He never came to and passed on in the ambulance. It was Carl's fault. He'd crossed the line and smacked into a box truck, spun and flipped over.

I remain quietly standing, watching a squirrel climb up a skinny pine tree. How long should I wait before I can turn back and tell Mr. Palczynski there's nothing out here? No voices, no howlings.

I report to Ralph that I've found nothing, which is true, but the old guy isn't satisfied. "No disrespect, but you didn't look hard enough."

The sky is light now and I'm out of patience. "I'm sorry, sir."

"Maybe I'll go look myself."

"I don't recommend it."

He waves his hand dismissively at me.

Fifteen minutes later I'm pulling away in my patrol car. An hour later I'm home in bed, the blinds drawn but the sun is too bright. Rays cut through the chinks. I flop over and drape an old blue T-shirt over my eyes to make it dark, but I'm pestered with images of Ralph traipsing through the woods, tripping over a branch and getting himself into a bad situation. Yet more than that, the old guy's voice batters my thoughts and I start to think he's right—that perhaps the young officer hadn't gone deep enough into the woods, that there is something out there.

"Hell," I grumble and get up.

I choose not to take my patrol car because it won't get through the sand and technically, I am off duty. Instead, I drive Carl's Subaru along Route 70. The Honda Carl crashed had been mine, so now I use his vehicle. I'm still finding things like old gum wrappers or receipts for gas—things that were once his.

I stop at a traffic light and stare, noticing a light strand of hair caught between the glass and the dashboard. I reach forward and grab it—it's a thread of Carl's blond hair. He wore it long. He played bass in a local band that did covers—Allman Brothers, Grateful Dead, Springsteen. "What about your band?" I had asked him, referring to our never-ending debate about North Carolina.

"I'll find another."

My head hurts just thinking about it. I roll down the window and drop the strand into the air. The light turns green and I drive, veering off Route 70 onto one of the back county roads, following it until I locate what I'm looking for.

The dirt fire trail is firm and packed hard in the beginning. But as I move along, it becomes soft—Pine Barrens sugar sand—and I put the Subaru in all-wheel drive. I travel slowly, maneuvering the vehicle more towards the side of the road, where the terrain is a little tougher. Even with the air conditioner running and the windows closed, the faint drone of insects seep into my ears. I drive around a bend and then another, the morning sun shining fiercely. A rabbit dashes across the road. Desolation hangs heavily in my soul.

I go and go, hope and relief inching quickly in my skin—I'm wrong, thank God. There's no one here and after each bend, I promise myself I'm going to turn around, head home, put my head down on my pillow.

Then I see it—a large white sedan. My heart sinks as I drive the Subaru closer until I brake, making sure what I'm seeing is real. I find my cell and get out of the car. As I walk towards the white vehicle, I phone the police station.

"Why are you out there alone?" Rick Olsen from dispatch says. "Hell, why are you out there in the first place?"

"Just send someone. Ambulance too."

After I hang up, I begin to run, and just like when I'd come upon Carl's accident, my heart rips through the beats: hard, heavy, fast.

The soft sand makes it difficult to reach the car quickly. The sounds of insects pierce in my ears, the morning sun blazes. The air is thick with heat.

Both car doors are open.

An elderly woman is in the passenger seat, motionless, stiff. Her eyes are closed, her mouth slightly open, her lips cracked. Dry blood is under her nose. When I touch her wrist for a pulse, the skin is lifeless. Dead. I step back and examine the tires—they are mired in the sand. My eyes snap back to the woman. I notice her white shoes are covered in gray sand and bits of it dot her bare, elderly legs. I see the dull gold wedding band is tight on her finger. Three green-head flies sit in her hair. She had a husband with her, didn't she? The driver.

I glance around. Where is the driver? I wander a few paces in front of the car, stop, stare north, look through the warped thin trunks of pine and white oak trees. A green-head stalks me and I brush it away, but it is relentless, buzzing at my ear. Ralph's house would be a few minutes' walk through the forest. Where the hell could the driver be?

I hike along the sandy road, gazing through the southern part of the woods. Nothing. Sweat pools in my bra, drips down the side of my face. The green-head buzzes near my ear again. I return to the car and see the keys in the ignition. The fly bites my neck. "Fuck!" I growl, slapping my skin. "Fucking bastards!"

I make my way to the rear of the car and study the trunk. The guy couldn't be in there—could he? That would be nuts. Still, I go to the front, grab the keys, and return to open it. My stomach drops when I see what is inside: Food. Water. Milk—all untouched. Immediately my fist goes to my mouth and I breathe heavily into it. The sun rages over my body.

I grab a gallon of water from one of the bags and hike through the sand, calling out to the driver. "Hello? Hello! I'm here to help! Hello!"

Nothing. I hear the faint sound of sirens in the distance. "Hello!" I yell again.

I go into the north woods, scrambling through the brush, calling out desperately to the driver.

"Hello! You there?" I assume he's under shade. Maybe.

"Hello!" I yell again.

There is movement. I stop. Spin around, and again. Twenty feet away I see the figure on the ground, propped up against a pine tree like an oversized discarded puppet. I rush towards him.

"Sir, are you okay?" I call, bending down.

The elderly man is bad, yet alive. His eyes look at me but his body does not move. I quickly open the water gallon and attempt to pour a little into the man's mouth. It only drips down his chin, onto his shirt.

"Sir?" I feel for a pulse but it is barely there. "Sir? Stay with me. An ambulance is on the way. Do you understand? An ambulance is on the way."

The man blinks weakly but says nothing, moves nothing.

Hours later, I pay a visit to Ralph Palczynski. "You were right." I tell him about the couple, how they must have grown disoriented and dehydrated, not realizing they had water in the trunk. The man in the woods had passed on in the ambulance.

"Yeah, I seen that happen," Ralph says. "But there comes a point when the body can't take food or liquid and they leave the earth. Such a terrible twist of fate."

I think about it for a long moment, remember

that he probably experienced some of this in the war. "That must've been rough to see as a young man," I say.

Ralph waves his hand. "Nah. I was tough. You gotta be tough in life."

Before I leave, Ralph reminds me that he isn't crazy. "I told you. I ain't half-gone like a lot of these folks. You had to be out of your mind in the first place to drive out into the middle of the Pine Barrens and not notice you ain't near your goddamn home. That's what I call crazy. The wife, too, for not making him turn around."

I don't work that night. I just sit at the kitchen table, drinking a two-month-old Budweiser. The twelve-pack had never been finished, something Carl had brought home the weekend before he died—I have left most of his things as is. I sip the beer and think about the woman in the car, her dead pulse and the dried blood under her nose. The detective told me that the couple had been married for fifty years.

I lean back in my chair and think about Carl, how I desperately want to tell him the story, and how I want to cry. But I don't cry. I just drink my beer and wonder how you can hate someone and miss them all at the same time. How could my husband have been so stupid to cross into the other lane? Why hadn't he been more careful? Sure, my job is usually mundane—traffic stops, teenagers fooling around. But every so often something terrible crops up—the crippled father beaten with a wrench by his son, the high school girl raped by her boyfriend's cousin, the toddler who drowned in the pool. The old couple who died in the woods.

"My little cop," Carl used to whisper when I'd crawl into bed in the mornings. He had a way of pulling me close and helping me fall asleep, even with the rays of sun piercing through the chinks in the window shades.

Previously published in Beat to a Pulp.

PIPE

Tyrell Colton, fourteen, a skinny black kid, one of the smallest students in the freshman class, woke at five-thirty on a Wednesday morning, leaned over the side of the mattress and pulled a two-inch wide, two-foot long pipe the color of gunmetal from underneath his bed. He lay back against his pillow and twirled it in his hands. The radio was on low and the murmuring of Grandmaster Flash segueing into Van Halen gently filled the room.

After a few minutes, Tyrell stood, set himself into a stance, and held the pipe forward with both hands like a medieval weapon. He swung it into space, a phantom enemy before him. Back and forth, back and forth.

Eventually, the boy dressed in jeans, white sneakers, a gray sweatshirt, and attached a digital watch on his wrist. He brushed his teeth in the bathroom, stole two of his mother's cigarettes and a pack of matches. Then he put on his father's green army jacket. Edward Colton had survived a two-year tour of Vietnam but he couldn't survive regular life. Shot himself four years earlier in '79 when Tyrell was eleven.

When Tyrell got outside, the morning sky was

heavy with mean, gray clouds. Icy drizzle flecked against his face as he hiked down the street, his stride quick, the pipe hidden in his jacket, the one end tucked into an inside pocket while the rest rose underneath his coat and against his torso until it reached his shoulder blade.

The kids from Tyrell's neighborhood were the only ones who walked to the high school. Every morning they'd tromp to the far right corner of the development, turn onto a wide orange-tinted dirt road and follow it until they reached the paved street which would take them to the high school. The brown brick building sat before a wide field of dry grass and weeds, surrounded by pine barren trees, and beyond that, abandoned cranberry bogs. When Tyrell and the kids walked along the paved road, yellow buses sped by, the growling motors piercing the walkers' ears. Usually someone inside a bus would press their hand against a window and flip them the bird.

But on this morning, Tyrell didn't take the regular way. He went beyond the orange dirt road, favoring a trail through the woods. Most of the path was thick with gray sugar sand that was difficult to walk through—not a popular way to go to school unless there was a joint to be smoked. Tyrell didn't think he'd meet anyone this early, and he skirted along the sides of the sand trail where the terrain was harder, letting pine tree branches slap against the army coat. Sometimes, when the moment was right, Tyrell could smell his father in this jacket—an odor of man's skin, cigarette smoke, kerosene. His father had spent many nights in the garage, sitting with liquor and a portable heater.

The pipe was riding against his shoulder blade, so Tyrell stopped, opened his coat and took the pipe out. He found his mother's cigarettes and attempted to light one with a match. The drizzle had stopped but it was still cold and windy. After three tries, the cigarette was lit, and Tyrell stood in nature, feeling the harshness of smoke in his lungs, becoming lightheaded. He watched a cardinal flutter from tree to tree, its red coat pretty against the dull browns, tans, and dreary greens of the scrub pine forest.

Tyrell reviewed his plan. He'd get to school before the buses, before he had to walk through the knots of students—the girls with their feathered hair and tight jeans, smoking cigarettes and cackling; the guys wearing camouflage jackets, dip tucked under their bottom lips, spitting the tobacco into plastic cups or onto the concrete patio of the school. There were black kids and Puerto Rican kids, too, and they hung out with their boom boxes on the edge of the patio, leaning against the brown brick walls, playing rap music, raising the volume after one of the guys with a lump of Skoal in his mouth would shout, "Shut that shit off, asshole!"

Tyrell had few friends. Ever since his father had killed himself, he'd been branded as strange, damaged, cursed. He was a quiet kid, never in trouble, good at math, a secret lover of all things science fiction but not obsessed with it. He had a crush on Iris Cruz, the pretty girl from New York whose parents spoke only Spanish.

He dropped the cigarette into the sand and thought about smoking the second one, but that was part of the plan, too. That was the victory cigarette, after he beat the shit out of Mark Horak with his pipe.

Tyrell looked at his watch: 6:46. Homeroom began at 7:22. He placed the pipe in his coat and began to walk again. He'd go into school early, put his jacket and pipe in his locker, and then head over to the library to hide out until the early morning bell. When it was time, he'd take the long way around to homeroom, then to first period. After first period ended, he'd head back to his locker, put on the jacket, sneak the pipe into the pocket, and slip into the bathroom near the science rooms. There he'd wait, eyeing his watch for the end of second period. Mark Horak always strolled by the bathroom at the end of second period, sometimes with his buddies DJ Trout and Scott Parker, but more often Mark was by himself. Tyrell was betting on Mark being alone, and he planned to ambush the guy then.

If all three were together, this was a concern. DJ

Trout, with a full dark beard, was as wide and thick as any decent high school linebacker, which he was. Scott Parker was so pumped up on steroids, he looked like he'd pop and swirl around like a balloon if you stuck a pin in him. Mark was the smallest of the three, but by no means less threatening. His hands were large and strong, as Tyrell had found out last Thursday when Mark slammed the boy up against the bulletin board in the hallway outside the French classroom, right hand clasped around Tyrell's little neck, choking him, the French teacher screaming. Fear had ripped through Tyrell and he felt tears drip from the far corners of his eyes. *Please don't,* he thought. *Please don't kill me.*

It took the vice principal, Mr. Cage, to pull Mark off Tyrell. The man came flying around the corner like a superhero, wrapped his right arm around Mark's neck and wrenched him away in one jolt. Mr. Cage was a strong, big man. He had a long face, wore square brown-framed glasses, and had a thick dark mustache like bicycle handles. He towered over the students like a giant. It was said he'd killed eighty-three people in Vietnam.

"I've had enough of you, Mr. Horak," Mr. Cage growled, tossing Mark across the hall.

Mark, huffing and snarling, glared at the vice principal.

Mr. Cage stepped up to the teenager and pointed his finger in the kid's face. "You need to keep your garbage in check. Now move it."

As he escorted Mark away, Mr. Cage turned and nodded at Tyrell, and this made the boy feel good, vindicated. The French teacher, clearly upset, approached him, put her hand on his shoulder and suggested he go to the nurse. But Tyrell declined, rubbing his neck, relieved the vice principal had saved him. Mr. Cage must've been a brave soldier, Tyrell thought as he walked to his next class. Someone you could count on to watch your back.

Mark was suspended for the incident, put out for three days. But Tyrell knew that when he returned on Wednesday, the guy planned to hunt Tyrell down and beat him to a pulp. He knew this because Janine Finn, a ghostly white girl with long black, witchy hair, who was one of the school sluts and known for knowing things, had secretly warned him.

"Don't you got some brothers to help you out?" she whispered.

Tyrell had no siblings and it took a minute, but he realized she meant other black people.

"I'll figure it out," he said.

"I understand you got to stand up for yourself when he ranks on you," she said. "But you gotta know when you retaliate, when you run your mouth, he's gonna get physical."

Since the beginning of the year, Tyrell had been one of Mark's targets. So had a little dorky kid with a bunch of freckles named Loren. "Loren. Ain't that a girl's name? I know you're confused.

Sneak into your sister's room and put on her pantyhose, don't you?" Overweight Marcy Puckett was another one. "You're so fat, we should send you to Ethiopia and have them cook you." And Lawrence Hawkins, a black kid who was strong and built himself, yet cursed with a feeble brain. He shot back at Mark, but his retorts were stupid and they only made Mark and the kids around him laugh. Teachers yelled at Mark, tried to defend the weak, but there were always lulls, moments, distractions opening up opportunities.

That Thursday, right before the choking went down, Mark had chosen Tyrell to pick on. Just saw him in the hall and sang this jingle: *"If I had a son like you, I'd a killed myself too."*

Tyrell, who'd heard Mark's jingle a half-dozen times before, got some nerve up, turned and said, "Your dad makes you suck his dick." The words fired from his mouth without edit, without gates, like he'd accidently hit the trigger of a machine gun and sent seven bullets into a crowd.

When Tyrell emerged from the woods, the school lay before him like a fortress. 7:01. He walked steadily along the paved road, careful to keep the pipe hidden, his stomach clenched with anticipation. Teachers in their cars passed by. He went across the empty patio, stepping around old spots of brown spit. Inside the building, he followed his plan: locker, stash coat and pipe, library.

In the large room with its rectangular tinted windows, Tyrell picked up *Mad Magazine* and sat at one of the cubby desks, careful to keep his head down. It was unlikely Mark would come to the library, but Tyrell didn't want to take chances. He turned the magazine's pages but read and saw nothing, only felt the tightness in his blood and bones that controlled anxiety brought on. When the bell rang, the plan continued. He traveled the long way to homeroom, sat quietly, and then on to first period English. They read and discussed *Antigone*.

Tyrell had left the pipe in the jacket and after first period, as he stood at his locker with other kids, he found it tricky to get the coat on without the pipe falling out. Yet somehow he managed and as he walked to the designated bathroom, he prayed he would not run into Mr. Cage.

When he arrived, Tyrell made his way into a stall, locked the door, and sat down on the toilet.

He pulled up his sleeve and checked his watch. Then he waited. Read some of the graffiti written or carved into the brown walls. *Fuck You, Mr. Petti is a Dick, Black Sabbath, Judas Priest, 666.* There were several drawings of pentagrams.

The main door to the bathroom was always propped open by the custodians, a trick to keep the smokers from smoking cigarettes. But halfway through second period, two kids came in and smoked anyhow. They barely spoke, just talked briefly about a job at McDonald's one of them had just scored. If they noticed Tyrell was in the stall, they said nothing. Just left.

Eventually, the time arrived. Tyrell pulled the pipe out of his father's jacket, then stared at his watch, waited, heard the bell ring.

He breathed, gripped the pipe in his left hand, his right hand on the stall lock. He studied his watch, eyes following the second counter, his heart punching, his breath short. The plan was to leave the stall at the end of the first minute, whether someone entered the bathroom or not.

Fifty-six, fifty-seven, fifty-eight, fifty-nine... Tyrell opened the door and stepped out. Luck was with him—he was alone. He crept to the doorway, leaned against the propped open door, clasping his pipe like a baseball bat. A girl walked by and another, but neither of them noticed him. These girls were more luck, though, because Mark Horak called to them. Tyrell was able to hear his location, enabling the oncoming attack to occur at the perfect time.

Go.

He burst out into the hallway swinging, smashing the pipe against Mark's shoulder, making the guy bend forward, shout in pain. Tyrell swung again, downwards this time, striking him on the back. Mark cried out again but did not fall. Tyrell swung once more, at the kneecap. His enemy finally collapsed to the floor, sobbing like a small child.

Tyrell took another swipe, at the face now, busting the nose, blood exploding in dots and splatters like boiling sauce on the stove. The guy begged for mercy, *"Stop, stop!"* and Tyrell did. He stood for a moment, breathing, staring at his work, gripping the pipe. He looked up, saw three kids—one girl and two guys—watching.

"Holy shit," said the girl.

Tyrell heard the voice of the vice principal and this kicked him out of his stupor. He took off, bolting down the hallway, around the corner, and out through the glass doors. He heard the doors open behind him and the VP shouting for him to stop. Even though Mr. Cage was large and strong, he was a little round about the middle, and he smoked, and he was older—it wouldn't be long before the man would have to stop, so Tyrell kept going. He raced across the patio, onto the road, then into the field, hoping his pursuer might fall in the grass. Halfway through the field, Tyrell looked back and saw that Mr. Cage had stopped on the patio, but Tyrell continued to run. He raced into to the woods, to the trail he'd come through in the morning, and once he was deep down the path, he slowed down to a jog, and then to a walk, the pipe still in his hand.

His chest was heaving so he let himself catch his breath. For the moment, he was safe. Soon they'd call the police, perhaps have a manhunt out for him. Maybe they'd just go to his house, wait for him to come home. Either way, there was no way around it—he was going to get caught.

Tyrell stopped walking and listened for the search. No noise except the wind moving the trees, the cold breeze cooling his heated face. Tyrell stared at the weapon, looked for blood from Mark's busted nose. Nothing.

He should've packed a bag with money, hidden it in the woods, prepared a getaway plan. He had cousins in Baltimore, an uncle in Lancaster, Pennsylvania. It would have taken him hours, but he could've walked to the bus station in Toms River, bought a ticket. Or he could have walked to the drug store on 37, called one of the taxis the old people always used, got a ride to the station. Once at his final destination, he'd phone his mother. Maybe she would quit her job and move to Baltimore or Lancaster. So many possibilities.

The cardinal appeared again, or maybe it was a different cardinal. Tyrell watched it for a moment as it flitted from pine tree to pine tree, trees so thin and scrawny and short, they were useless for anything like climbing or making forts. As the red bird darted here and there, Tyrell noticed a narrow path through the woods. It was so thin and covered with golden pine needles, that it was hardly detectable.

Tyrell took the path.

It looped and coiled through the forest, his steps crunching against the pine needles. Some of the path was heavy sand, some of it hard black dirt. Maybe it was an old Indian trail, he thought, and his mind went there, daydreaming that he was an Indian, his bow and arrow in his hands, other companions in front of him, behind him. Tyrell's father had walked through the jungles of Vietnam like that, holding machine guns, watching the trees for snipers.

Within minutes the narrow trail opened into a huge square hole of stagnant water with patches of brown foliage growing on top of it—an abandoned cranberry bog. Tyrell found a log to sit on, put his pipe down, and lit his second cigarette. Again, the smoke pained his lungs and he became lightheaded, but this time he enjoyed the sensation. Trees swished in the chilly wind and the sky was still gray. Tyrell wondered if he had killed Mark. Then he wondered how his father would've felt about the beating. Would he have been proud? Would he have been angry?

Tyrell looked at his watch—it was still second period. Time went so slow, and he began to grow cold. After he finished the cigarette, he dropped it on the ground, squished it into the moist earth, kicked some dirt over it. Then he glanced at his pipe. In mob movies, they always dropped the gun. Drop the pipe. Tyrell picked it up and hurled it into the middle of the bog, watched it land near the brown foliage, glint in the gray light before it somehow sank.

There was nowhere to go but home, so he turned and headed back the way he came.

When he hiked out of the narrow path and turned onto the main trail, there, about thirty feet away, stood a tall, dark-haired man. Mr. Cage. Tyrell immediately stopped, tried to think of what to do, blood shooting into his brain, but the vice principal spun around and spotted him.

"Tyrell Colton!" he called. "Don't run. They're waiting for you at both ends."

It seemed like a lie, but Tyrell wasn't sure. He didn't move.

Mr. Cage tromped along the path until he stood a foot away from the boy.

Tyrell asked, "Who's waiting for me?"

"Mark's friends. You know, DJ Trout and Scott Parker." Mr. Cage stared down at Tyrell. His ugly square glasses magnified his eyeballs absurdly.

"No police?"

Mr. Cage shook his head. "No. We didn't call the police."

The boy looked at the ground. He didn't really believe Mr. Cage, even though he wanted to.

"You better walk with me. Come back to the school. You'll be safer."

"You got something to keep me safe? Like a gun?"

Mr. Cage rubbed his mustache with his hand.

"Those boys won't get in between me and you. You know that."

In the distance, the sound of the school's bell rang.

"Let's go, son," Mr. Cage said. "We'll figure this out."

Tyrell wanted to trust the man. After all, he'd shot eighty-three people in Vietnam. He knew right from wrong, being a soldier.

"Come on. I'll help you."

"How?"

"We'll figure it out. Let's go."

Tyrell said okay and Mr. Cage stepped back, letting the boy go ahead of him. After a few paces, the vice principal and Tyrell were side by side, Mr. Cage trekking through the soft sugar sand, Tyrell walking along the edges. The school's bell rang again.

Then Mr. Cage suddenly stopped. "Hold on." He pulled off his brown left shoe, turned it over, and knocked something out of it. "Rock," he said, putting the shoe back on. Tyrell nodded, looked behind him. The path was deserted, quiet.

"Ready?"

"Yes," Tyrell said, and they began walking again.

"By the way," Mr. Cage asked, keeping his eyes cast down. "Where's the pipe? Because that's what it was, right?"

Tyrell didn't answer.

"Mr. Colton?"

"In the bog."

"Bog?"

Tyrell pointed south. "There's a bog back there."

Mr. Cage stopped walking, searched through the trees. "Which way?"

Tyrell also stopped and pointed again. The vice principal squinted his eyes, stared intensely. Then he glanced at Tyrell and cracked a smile. "A bog?"

"Yeah," Tyrell whispered.

Mr. Cage shook his head in wonderment. "Never knew that."

They resumed walking.

Near the end of the path, before the last bend, a cardinal flew overhead and landed on a tree branch. It watched, as if waiting for something to happen.

Tyrell stopped again. "You said they're waiting for me?"

Mr. Cage also stopped, turned, looked at the boy. The man shrugged. "No. Nobody's waiting for you."

"You lied?"

"Yes. So you'd come back to school and I could help you."

Tyrell thought about running but decided against it. Mr. Cage was a vice principal. They had to lie to kids sometimes to get them to do the right thing.

More than that, Tyrell wanted to believe Mr. Cage was going to help him.

"Let's go, son."

"What's gonna happen to me?"

"Nothing much. We'll figure it out."

Tyrell hesitated. He wanted to explain. "I was defending myself."

"I know."

Tyrell glanced into the woods and his eyes caught the cardinal flying away.

Mr. Cage said, "Okay, son. We have to go."

Tyrell was still hesitant and he thought hard about what his father would do. He tried to summon the man in heaven and appealed for an answer.

Nothing came.

"Mr. Colton," the vice principal said sternly.

Tyrell finally accepted that Mr. Cage wanted to do him good; that he'd come out here to help. The two began walking once more, making their way around the last bend. They stepped out of the trail, before the open field of the school.

And then they came at him, not like bullets or as they did on TV shows, but emerged, like secret guards in a castle, one from each side stepping from the shadows. Both wore blue uniforms, smelled of gum and coffee. They each hooked an arm, almost carrying the boy, and walked him to the car.

Tyrell heard one of the cops say something about assault and a weapon, but he wasn't really listening. Instead he looked back at Mr. Cage but the vice principal wasn't looking at him. The boy was sick to his stomach—he'd been so stupid to trust the man.

Still, he yelled out: "You said you were gonna help me!"

Mr. Cage shrugged.

"Why aren't you helping me?"

The cops cuffed Tyrell and then pushed him into the car.

"Why ain't he helping me?" Tyrell asked one of the police officers.

Later, through the window, Tyrell watched Mr. Cage speak briefly with another cop, nod, shove his hands in his pockets, and then walk across the field before the school. Like his father, he grew smaller as he went, and eventually and gently, disappearing.

Previously published in Thuglit.

METALHEAD MARTY
IN LOVE

Yeah, Marty was into metal. He loved it all: Priest, Scorpions, Maiden, Zeppelin, Metallica, Dio. The loud, violent music ruptured through his boom box before school, after school, the noise exploding in crackling dark beats and unending shouts and shrieks, taking Marty to dreamland, where he saw himself on an enormous stage, arms reaching out to him, voices begging for more.

In real life Marty Taylor had an electric guitar and a band that rehearsed in Phil Cone's garage, even though Phil was a crap-musician himself, but Marty and the rest of the guys had nowhere else to go, so they put up with the kid. And because Marty was so into playing guitar, and because he had that real potential—the stuff only few people were born with—one of his mother's boyfriends took him up to Old Bridge to hang out with Steve Palchak, an aging hippie-rocker dude, who'd been a roadie for Creedence and the Eagles, or so he claimed, and who had mad talent on every damn instrument he touched, and who played the bars in Asbury and Brighton Beach, and had jammed with Springsteen himself.

"You'll go far," Steve Palchak said after a few sessions with the teenager. "Just don't let a woman get in the way."

Women shouldn't have been a problem. Marty wasn't a handsome guy—he had long stringy hair like a true metalhead, but his face was rectangular shaped with sharp angles, and he had a terrible long, crooked nose. He was tall, skeletal, and his back was hunched—the guy almost looked like Nosferatu, except his eyes were little and he didn't have the same bushy black brows or fang teeth. So, yeah, if you were going on looks, he wasn't ever going to be one of the favorites of the local girls. On top of that, Marty came from one of those tough, low-class North Jersey families who'd moved down to desolate Ocean County because it was cheap. He lived in a decrepit house with his mother who sometimes had boyfriends move in and a mean-ass sister who repeatedly told him how fucking ugly he was. But despite this, despite the fact that his family was dirtbag city, despite the fact that he looked like a creepy vampire, Marty wasn't pissed off about it all, which meant he wasn't a dickhead. He kept to himself, strumming his guitar, dreaming his dreams, and had a mad quiet crush on Megan Tolly since the tenth grade, when he first set eyes on her, when she had just moved down from Roselle Park.

And that's the story here.

She drove him crazy. That long brown wavy

hair, those pretty blue eyes, freckles on her nose, freckles on her chest, just enough curves, a shy smile—a total fantasy for a guy like Marty. Sophomore year she sat in front of him in Geometry and because she sucked at math, she often turned around and asked for help. Marty pulled straight A's in that class because each night he took the book home and made sure he was on top of the next day's lesson, just in case she turned around and asked for assistance.

"I don't know what I'd do without you," she said over and over again.

He wrote songs about her but never had enough balls to bring them to the guys, so the words remained hidden in tattered notebooks under his mattress. And even though he said nothing to anyone about his crazy mad ache for Megan Tolly, pretty much everyone knew. Marty tried so hard not to watch when she crossed the lunchroom, tried so much not to help her each time her locker got stuck (they were across from one other), tried so much not to think about asking her out because he knew she'd shoot him down, like one of the local hunters sitting up in a tree, taking down a six-point buck.

Besides, it wasn't long before someone else noticed her. In the spring of sophomore year, Stuart Wade, a junior, started hanging around Megan's locker and day after day, Marty came upon them, making out or just looking at each other, she gazing at the guy, him grinning liked he'd won a dare. "I'll call you tonight," Stuart would say, and Marty, who just couldn't take it anymore, finally pulled his shit out of his locker and moved in with his mean-ass sister on the other side of the school.

"Why you gotta crowd me, ugly?" she said.

"Shut up," he told her.

His mother's boyfriend, the one who knew Steve Palchak, dropped out of the picture, but because Marty had a good after-school job at a gas station, he was able to buy a car and get up to Old Bridge to play with Steve. By the time Marty graduated high school, his band with Phil Cone and the rest of the guys had split up, and Marty was now a free agent. Steve put him in touch with some dudes from Howell and after a short audition, Marty was recruited to play lead guitar for the newly-formed Dark Beast.

"Fucking A, you play good!" the drummer hooted. "Like Tony Iommi!"

And it was true. Because when Marty played metal music—with all that mentoring from Steve Palchak and practice, and with that raw true-blue talent—it was like magic from some rock underworld. Dark Beast was absolutely thrilled they'd found him.

"You in a new band now?" his sister asked one night.

Marty beamed, proud of himself. "Yep."

It was obvious she was rip-roaring jealous. The girl was out of school, too, and she had nothing going for her. "I bet you guys suck."

Marty flipped her the bird.

After a few sessions with the guys, Marty got the nerve to pull out his songs about Megan Tolly. He wasn't much of a singer, but he sang for the group anyway:

"Deep holy hell, my heart is broke
Deep holy hell, my heart is toked
Deep holy hell, can't you see?
Oh, Baby, baby, you made a mess out of me."

The lead singer of Dark Beast, a handsome guy named Carmine Sardone, loved the lyrics, and he loved the intense riff Marty played, and with the drummer adding his slow, pummeling beats, the bass player adding the rhythm, the song, "Deep Holy Hell," became one of their flagship tunes, a favorite in the local bars they were playing gigs in.

Carmine asked for more, and Marty played "Witch with Dark Hair," "Hung," "Drawn and Quartered" (a song about Stuart Wade), and a metal ballad in the vein of Kiss's "Beth," but Marty called his "Meg."

* * *

Dark Beast was convinced they were going to hit the big time. It was 1988, the height of metal, and they were just a gig away from being discovered. Local music critics were writing good things, the following was getting bigger, and one night in February, while playing the Fastlane in Asbury, Marty looked out into the crowd and there, standing off to the right with Denise Mazziotti, was Megan Tolly. Marty was stunned, rocked. He missed a beat, Carmine shot him the evil-eye, and Marty looked down at his guitar, pulled himself back from the brink, and put that woman out of his mind.

After the show, when the band was outside loading up the van, before Marty could even search for them, Denise and Megan found him.

Denise, a hot number with teased-out hair, big boobs, and heavy makeup, a girl who never spoke to Marty in school, ran up and hugged him, said she couldn't believe he was in a band like Dark Beast, and could he introduce her to the lead singer?

"Damn, is he cute!" she squealed.

Marty swallowed, nodded, said hello to Megan.

"Hey, Marty," Megan said shyly. She was dressed in a black tube skirt, a thin black lacy sweater, and black boots with tassels in the back. Her legs were bare and she was shivering from the cold, her teeth chattering, and Marty so much wanted to do something about it.

"I got a long coat in my car, if you want," he offered.

"Oh, yeah?" she asked, her eyes brightening.

"Sure, hold on."

But Denise grabbed him first. "I mean it. Introduce me to him." She nodded towards Carmine, who was actually sneaking looks at her.

"Sure," he said impatiently, turning and calling out to Carmine, who smiled his sideways lead singer smile and strutted on over.

After Marty introduced the two, Megan tapped Marty on the arm. "Could you get me that coat?"

Marty nodded and ran in long lopes across the parking lot to his car. The coat was an old wool and gray tweed thing, something he'd found in the basement that had belonged to his dead grandfather, who, according to photographs, had also been tall, hunchbacked, and very thin.

When Marty returned, he noticed Megan had moved away from Denise and Carmine and was standing alone, her arms wrapped around herself. She grinned when she saw him and when he got to her, he held the coat out like a gentleman and Megan slipped into it. The sleeves were too long and the shoulders too wide but within a minute, she seemed much warmer.

"Thank you," she said quietly. A streetlamp shone over them and in the fluorescent beam, Megan's face was pale and ghostly, but ethereal, like she was in a Stevie Nicks video. Her lips were dark red, her long brown hair teased out a little, and she wore earrings in the shape of stars that glittered in the light.

"It's no problem," Marty muttered, looking away. The van was packed up and the guys were standing around, talking to girls who'd strolled up from the club. Carmine was telling a story and Denise was smiling, nodding, her head titled flirtatiously. Marty glanced at Megan and noticed she was watching her friend and the lead singer. Marty looked back at Carmine and Denise, just in time to see them kiss.

"Shit," Megan said, letting out a deep breath. "Now I'll never get home."

"I guess she drove you?" Marty asked.

"Yeah. She's not gonna leave now. Shit."

Marty braced himself. Megan was stranded. This was his moment.

"I can take you home."

Megan turned to him, relieved. "I would really, really appreciate that. Let me tell Denise." And with that, she darted over to the kissing couple.

In another moment, Marty and Megan were walking across the parking lot, Marty so wrecked with horror, so overwhelmed with joy, he couldn't speak. He remembered to open the door for her and apologized for any mess in the car, which there really wasn't. The car was a tank—a '76 gold Oldsmobile Cutlass—but it was in decent shape. As he walked around to the driver's side, he told himself he had to talk to her. He had to say something clever, amazing, something that might make her do this again.

"Are you hungry?" he asked when he started up the car.

"Yes."

As they drove, he asked her about math because she said she was attending OCC, Ocean County College, and she said she was bombing it like always. They went to a diner and he opened the glass door for her, let her walk in front of him when the waitress led them to their booth, helped her take off the coat.

They talked about what they wanted to eat— both wanted pancakes—and after the waitress took their order, a demon silence crawled up between them that Marty didn't know how to slay. What could he ask her now? Sure, the most normal person could come up with something but Marty was so nervous, he couldn't think of anything but: *Are you still with Stuart?*

And believe it or not, that's what he said.

Megan sighed. "He's up at Rutgers and he didn't bother with me much over Christmas break. So I drove to his house on New Year's Day because I didn't see him New Year's Eve. He's twenty-one now and he can go out to the bars, and I'm still twenty, so I can't. Anyway, he said he was hung over and he'd call me. Which he hasn't."

Marty nodded, because that's all he could manage.

Megan went on: "So now it's been almost a month. I guess he broke up with me."

"Maybe something happened."

"Like what? He got hit on the head and doesn't remember who he is? Shit. That may be a good thing."

Marty nodded again.

"Hell," she muttered, staring through the diner window. "I don't really care." Then she looked at him and he had to look away because his heart was flooded with hope.

"So your band is pretty good," she said. "I liked that song, 'Meg.'"

Marty desperately didn't want her to know the truth about the song, so he quickly kicked out a lie: "Yeah, Carmine used to have a girlfriend named Michelle but he didn't want her to know he wrote a song about her so he changed the girl's name to Meg."

Megan said, "Oh."

The pancakes arrived.

Later, after he pulled up in front of her house, she held out her hand to shake his. "Thanks."

He watched her run up the walkway to her front door, turn and wave before entering the house. Marty waved back, saw her go inside, then switched on the overhead light and peered into the rearview mirror. He looked okay, he thought. He was no Stuart Wade, with good looks and athleticism, or Carmine Sardone, with ego and lead singer sex appeal, but he could be a contender. He told himself that if Megan hadn't liked him even a little bit, meaning if she hated his guts, she would've called her dad or a neighbor to come pick her up and take her home. And she certainly wouldn't have eaten pancakes with him.

The good thing about Denise, according to Carmine, was that she knew how to screw. "She don't just lie there, you know?" This kept the lead singer happy and made Denise and Megan regular fans, not groupies, something more, classier. The girls came to every show, and at the end, Marty would take Megan to a diner and then he'd take her home. It became easier to talk to her and because she was so interested in his music, she asked him questions about how he wrote songs. One night, in the beginning of March, right in the diner, he came up with a tune and some lyrics and composed one right there.

"Wonderful!" she cried out and clapped.

Later, standing in front of his car, she stood up on her toes and kissed him. It was short and gentle, but a real kiss. He couldn't believe this was happening—his band was on the road to stardom, his dream girl was actually into him. The winter night was mild and Megan's top was low cut. They stood under a streetlamp and he placed his hand on the rim of her shirt, up towards her shoulders, but he stared at her freckled chest. He wanted to look into her eyes because he could feel her staring at him, but just couldn't.

"Kiss me back, Marty," she whispered.

He hesitated, almost choked.

"Marty?"

Finally, with a push from the gods, he leaned down and kissed her.

Marty never told Megan he loved her—never the right moment, too nervous, always putting it off to the next time.

He did ask her about Stuart, though. "Do you think he knows about us?"

"Maybe," Megan said quietly. They were in a motel room off of Route 35. Her head was resting under his chin, his left hand running up and down her bare arm.

"Have you talked to him?"

"No." She kissed his chest, then lifted her head and looked at Marty. "I'm going to give you some advice, okay?"

"Okay."

"Just watch your back."

"Why?"

"I don't know. Just in case he needs an excuse to beat someone up."

"He's like that?"

She sighed. "He could be."

The momentum of Dark Beast was in fifth gear now, like doing a hundred over the Seaside Bridge. Any day, any second, a man in a suit would come down from the city, flash a fancy New York contract, and sign them with a golden pen. "It's gonna happen," Carmine promised. "And you know this by the number of groupies that are waiting for you at the end of the night."

There were a lot of girls, and Carmine, being so handsome, couldn't turn down an easy blowjob. Denise stopped attending the shows but Megan didn't, making Marty sure of their relationship. With her in the crowd, every note sparked from his electric guitar, and the euphoric energy he put forth drove the rest of the guys to give it their all and the people cheered, especially when Marty leaned forward, played wildly, channeling Hendrix. Afterwards, girls would be waiting, offering to take each guy to the bathroom or to a dark corner, but Marty turned them down, knowing he had something better. And there she'd be: leaning against the wall, hands in her jacket pockets, tight short skirt, a leg crossed over another, wearing her tasseled boots, grinning.

"Kiss me, baby," she'd say, looking up at him.

Marry me, he wanted to say back, but never did.

* * *

In June, the romance suddenly fizzled. First, she said she couldn't come to a show. Had to take her mom somewhere. She went to the next one, but she was weird, claiming she had cramps and he had to drive her straight home after the gig.

"It's okay," Marty said, kissing her forehead before she got out of the car. "Get some rest."

"Thanks."

He watched her run up to her house, the moon wide and bright, shining on her figure as she went.

She wouldn't take his calls. He was sick, his guts tortured with pain, the grief ripping through his soul. What had he done? Why wouldn't she talk to him? The heartbreak showed up in his playing. He missed notes, the fire in his solos wasn't there, and Carmine pulled him aside.

"I know your girl ain't around no more, but you still have your music, man. For Christ's sake, get it fucking together!"

Marty got back on track. Carmine didn't shoot him the evil eye on stage, the riffs blew up again, but inside, Marty was destroyed. Each time Dark Beast played, Marty peered out into the crowd, hoping he'd seen her pretty face, hoping she would come back to him.

***

In July, they showed up after a gig in Toms River—Stuart Wade and two other idiots from school, Lou Eversham, who was a bulk of muscle, and John Kolowski, more muscle. With the band long gone, Marty had been alone in his car, writing lyrics about heartache, when Stuart and his guys banged on the window and ordered Marty outside.

Marty didn't move.

Stuart glared at him through the glass. "Be a man, asshole!"

Marty stepped out of the car. The parking lot was deserted, the bar shut for the night. It was a sight to see under the streetlamp—hunched-backed Marty with his long, stringy hair towering over the three muscle-heads like an anemic willow tree.

Stuart was piss-mad. He said he'd never broken up with Megan and when he ran into Marty's sister at the 7-Eleven the other night, he'd been surprised to find out that ugly Marty Taylor was banging his girlfriend.

"What do you have to say for yourself, dickweed?"

Marty didn't know how to answer. He shrugged, looked at the ground, looked back up at Stuart, decided to take the best way out—apologize. "I'm sorry, man. I thought you two had split. Honestly."

"She tell you that?"

Not wanting to betray Megan, not wanting to

explain that she had said she didn't give a shit about Stuart and that she was single and free to be with whomever she wanted, that she had said that to Marty after that first kiss, because he'd asked her that night, right before he took her to the motel, and she said so—but Marty told Stuart no. "I never asked her. I just assumed."

"So you never thought to say, 'Do you have a boyfriend?'"

"No. I'm sorry, man."

Stuart looked at his dudes and shook his head. "You're a fucking asshole."

And with that, Stuart lunged forward, swung, hit, knocked Marty against his car, battered his face with two more punches. Marty slipped to the ground, his tall skeletal body no match for the strength Stuart possessed.

Stuart watched Marty as he coiled up in pain.

"You're such a fucking idiot!" Stuart barked. "You think she really wanted you? As soon as I called her, she came running back."

Marty stared up at Stuart, finally comprehending why Megan disappeared from his life. "So you called her in June, right?"

Stuart said yes. "Then I drove to her house and she jumped in my car, dickhead."

Marty nodded, let his head come to rest on the ground. His face was sore from the punches, but it was his heart and ego that ached more.

Then this happened: suddenly, out of nowhere,

Lou Eversham grunted, stepped forward, and kicked the poor guy in the stomach. Marty rolled over, moaned, begged for it to stop, his left hand swinging out for a moment, slapping against the blacktop. It lay out there, waiting, and Lou delivered the final blow—he lifted his booted right foot and stomped on Marty's left hand, crushing the finger bones like they were sticks.

For a brief moment, Stuart watched Marty cradle his broken hand, groan in pain and sadness, and you had to believe something in that boy understood he'd done bad.

Marty didn't have health insurance so he didn't get the best care. And it turned out, Marty had a disease that caused brittle bones—which made the injury catastrophic. His fingers were mangled and crushed, the thumb wrecked. The doctors had no choice but to amputate everything and leave nothing but a nub.

For three months, Dark Beast held out for a miracle, the guys coming to the hospital, visiting Marty at home, cheering him on, saying he'd play again, just look at Rick Allen of Def Leppard, who after his accident, was playing the drums with one arm! Even Tony Iommi, who'd had the tops of his fingers cut off in a sheet metal accident, could still play guitar. But Marty's situation was much worse. The amputation, they all knew, signaled that this was the end, the end of Marty's career, the end of Dark Beast.

Megan moved away. Her parents sold their house and she went with them. Virginia or North Carolina, Marty's mean-ass sister said.

"I'm so sorry I told Stuart about you and Megan," she whined. "I thought he knew."

Marty, sitting in a lawn chair on his patio, sipped a beer and shrugged, then told her to fuck off.

It didn't matter, he thought, looking up into a gray sky. The world was useless, the gods were cruel.

Rain fell on his face.

Years later, when there is Google and Facebook, a reflective Megan, divorced with two kids, looks for Marty Taylor, just to see how he is doing, or so she tells herself. These days, the memories of him bounce around her head, and the more she thinks of him, the more she compares him to Stuart, to the other guys who came after him, to her ex-husband, to the men who followed her divorce. But Marty is nowhere to be found. She sends Carmine Sardone a Facebook message. He doesn't reply. So she writes Marty's sister, but the guy's whereabouts are a mystery. "We haven't heard from him in years," answers the sister. "He could be dead for all we know."

And one evening, while sitting on her deck, sipping her Pinot, watching the last of the lightening bugs fade out, her pretty face growing old, Megan finally realizes that the only man who would ever love her like Marty Taylor did, was Marty Taylor. Most men, although they wanted love—claimed they'd climb mountains and fight giants for a taste—didn't have it in them to love one woman, solely, faithfully, heart, gut, mind, like Marty loved Megan. She realizes it had been a gift, a treasure from the gods, a comet, a mermaid, a Pegasus. Oh, how she wants it back.

Oh, how her soul hurts.

Previously published in Yellow Mama.

JUNE

June, wearing a worn yellow eyelet dress, sat in front of the radio, listening to the Velvelettes sing "A Needle in a Haystack." The music almost drowned out the noise coming from the bedroom, her mother and Mr. Gash back there, wood bedframe banging against the wall, the grunts from him.

The apartment was small—just the bedroom and the front room, a kitchenette off to the side. The men came by, not often, but they came, and in the past, June would go outside and play in the dirt lot next to the building. Today she didn't. She was getting older, figuring things out, and these men, in their dungarees or slacks, always with wrinkled shirts, cigarettes hanging from their mouths, they arrived at all hours, sometimes standing in the kitchenette, taking a nip of whiskey before disappearing into the bedroom with her mother.

Once, June overheard Mrs. Lambstock, the landlady, talking with Mr. Pratt, who lived below. "It ain't no business of mine what she does," the woman said. "As long as she pays the rent."

Mr. Gash carried a leather wallet and at the moment, it sat on the small card table where June and her mother ate their meals. The banging kept going and the girl moved her ear closer to the radio. She tried to think of other things, like a piece of chocolate cake from the bakery on the main street, or watching television at Betty Kecher's house, or learning about colonial times in school from her teacher. But none of it removed the thought that Mr. Gash was in the bedroom, that his dented-up car sat in front of the building, everyone knowing why he was there.

She turned around, stared at the card table, her eyes finding the wallet. She knew there was money in it. Probably with other things, like crinkled photographs of his girlfriend or his wife, maybe his kids. She didn't know much about Mr. Gash. He came from another place, her mother said. "I don't know where he lives. Don't care much."

June hadn't eaten since the day before, for there was nothing in the apartment. Her mother had promised that after Mr. Gash left, she'd take her down to the market and they'd buy a chicken and a couple of potatoes. The girl's stomach ached terribly, and she licked her lips, thinking that the bakery may be open still, that with a little money she'd be able to buy something, perhaps a roll.

Carefully, June stood up, the banging from the bedroom thrashing in fast steady beats, *boom, boom, boom,* and she crept to the card table, picked up the wallet, opened it. Her breath stopped when she noticed the bills—so many ones, fives, tens. She pulled the money out, looked at it, thought of all the things she could buy: a whole cake, several rolls, a record player. She placed the wallet down, folded up the cash in her hands, turned for the door. But the banging suddenly stopped, followed by a great long howl. June froze, her brain trying to think, stay or go, stay or go. When he finished, Mr. Gash always emerged from the bedroom rather quickly, half-dressed—shoes untied, shirt unbuttoned, belt unhooked and hanging from his waist. There's no way she could get down the three flights of wooden stairs and make a run for it through the streets. So she returned to her spot on the floor in front of the radio, her legs crossed Indian style, her back facing the bedroom door. The song had long moved to something else, Elvis maybe, but she wasn't hearing it. The money was in her hand and she straightened the bills out, shoved them underneath the rug.

The bedroom door opened.

"Turn that noise down," Mr. Gash barked. June immediately obeyed, reaching up, moving the knob so the music was lower, keeping her back to the man. She heard him walking along the floorboards, coughing, groaning like he had some terrible ache, muttering about more whiskey. She heard the pouring of the drink, his gulp, the glass hitting the metal counter by the sink. June stared at the small rise in the carpet where the bills were hidden. Any moment he'd realize his money was gone.

"What's this?" he said.

June kept steady.

"What the hell is this?" he said again, and June felt the floor shake as he walked towards her. In a second, his untied brown shoes were inches away from her face.

"You take my money?" he growled.

"No," she said, keeping her eyes down.

"Girl, you look at me!"

June hesitantly turned and peered up at him. He was staring down at her like a beast, holding his empty wallet, his face pink and raw, glistening with sweat.

"Where's my money?"

She shook her head. "I don't know."

"Bullshit. You do know."

"I don't."

"What? You blaming it on your mom, then? You saying she stole it?"

"No."

"Then you stole it, didn't ya?"

"No."

June saw her mother, wearing a gray satin robe, appear from the bedroom. Her hair was messy and she was barefoot.

"What's the matter?" she asked, padding across the room and standing next to Mr. Gash.

"Your kid took my money," he said.

She placed her hands on her hips. "Is he right?"

"No," June whimpered.

"You go in his wallet?"

She said nothing, just sat on the floor, looking up at her mother.

"Tell me!"

Finally June answered. "Yes."

Like the snap of a whip, June's mother lunged forward, snatched her daughter by the arm and wrenched her up. June tried to squirm away, but her mother had a firm hold. She grabbed June by the mouth and squeezed so hard the girl's teeth hurt.

"You show me now!"

June pointed to the small bump in the carpet. Immediately, Mr. Gash bent down, flung the rug over and grabbed his money. The woman let go of her daughter's face and pushed the child away. June rubbed her mouth with her hand. Both watched Mr. Gash count the bills.

"I'm missing ten bucks," he said.

"No you ain't!" June cried. "I didn't hide it anywhere else."

Mr. Gash shoved the money in his wallet and stomped across the room, towards the front door.

"June!" her mother hollered. "Where's the rest?"

The girl shook her head. "I didn't hide money anywhere else. Just there, under the rug."

The woman studied her daughter for a long moment before turning to Mr. Gash. "She ain't lying, Al. I can see it in her face."

Mr. Gash sucked on his lips, shrugged.

"You got to pay, Al. You know that."

He opened the front door. "No, I don't."

"Al! You owe me money!"

Mr. Gash ignored June's mother and left, slamming the door behind him.

"Al!" she screamed. "Goddammit! You no good son of a bitch!"

Then she swung around and turned her rage on her daughter.

"You think that radio gets played by air? You think money grows on the goddamn trees?"

June began to weep.

"Damn, girl! Now we got nothing! Nothing!" She beat June across the face with an open hand. One hit, another hit, another.

Later, her mother fixed soup from a can, something she went and got from Mr. Pratt down below, and made June sit at the table and watch her eat it. June's face was still sore from the beating, pain shooting into the top of her head, but it was her stomach that hurt more—how hungry she was.

With each slurp, her mother hummed, smiled, licked her teeth. "Oh, so tasty," she crooned.

She finished every last bit and made her daughter wash the bowl.

Previously published in Flash Fiction Offensive/Out of the Gutter 8.

CIRCLING

We grew up two miles away from each other, both in small houses, not far from where the great Hindenburg circled and crashed a million years ago.

"Andrea, I'm in deeper shit than this," Michael McMurran says, his body and head facing the dirt, hands pulled back in cuffs.

I'm not in the mood to deal with him. My husband's death is still recent and my stamina for dealing with crap is at an all-time low. I stand straight in my gray uniform, looking down at Michael, saying nothing.

"This is nothing," he mutters. "I got bigger problems."

"Yeah? You think I care?" That's the other cop, my new partner, Jenkins. He's young, skinny, the boss's nephew, not cut out for the occupation of policeman. The kid is hotheaded and a touch twisted. He enjoys scaring senior citizens when he pulls them over—*you know I can have your license revoked.* I was asked to take him under my wing.

"This ain't nothing," Michael mumbles again.

"Close your mouth," Jenkins snaps. "I'm tired of dealing with you already!" Even in the muddy glow of the overhead light from the police car, I can see the young guy redden.

"Officer," I say calmly. It's code to remind him: *Do not engage.*

"You've been dealing with me for all of ten fucking minutes!" Michael barks.

Jenkins is infuriated: "Didn't I tell you to be quiet? You better watch that language and show respect."

Michael lifts his head, twisting towards the twenty-four-year-old cop. "What are you? Fucking in the seventh grade and all of eighty pounds? Hell, I'll kick your ass all the way down to Atlantic City."

"Mike," I say. "Put a lid on it."

Michael doesn't. He keeps going, mumbling crap. "Damn kids. Think they're tough because they got a cop job. It's nothing but a job." He raises his head off the ground even higher, screwing his neck back until his veins protrude like miniature cables. He scowls at my red-faced skinny partner. "You hear? Ain't nothing but a goddamn job!"

Jenkins glares at me. The young cop is at a loss and piss angry about it. His hands ball up.

"Mike," I say. "Put your head down and take a breather." I direct Jenkins to go inside and get the woman of the house to make a report. She was outside earlier, screaming her head off until her best friend arrived, ushering her inside.

"Fine," the young cop grunts. "Whatever." He

turns and hikes across the front yard until he reaches the concrete porch of the small, squat ranch. The door opens and he goes in.

I look around the area. The house is at a dead end, encircled by dark woods. The aroma of pine sap, sandy dirt, and brush soak the night's air. I grew up a few blocks away. "You living here, Mike?"

"Just staying for a bit." The left side of Michael's head is fully resting on the ground. He's worn himself out by yelling and now, when he speaks, it's with difficulty and into the earth. "It was Julie's mother's house. Her mom's living with her sister."

"So it's Julie's house now?"

"I guess." Michael raises his head again. "I don't ask her questions much. Turns into a long-ass story I ain't prepared to listen to."

I chuckle. The guy can still make me laugh. "All right. I'm gonna sit you up."

"Cool."

I bend down and help Michael turn and sit on the cracked cement curb. His hands are still behind his back and he rubs his cheek against his shoulder to take the dirt off his face.

"I could use a smoke," Michael says when he sorts himself out.

"Can't help ya."

"I ain't asking, I'm just saying."

I watch as Michael lets out a deep breath, looks

into space. The man is in sweat pants and a Mets T-shirt and white socks, his head is shaved, and a thin gold chain with a cross hangs around his neck. His chest is wide, the arms muscular, every part of him dense, like an old boxer.

"They're coming to get me, tonight," Michael says, looking up at me. "So, even if it's crazy to say, I'm real glad you're here."

I want to roll my eyes. "Your gambling out of control again?"

Mike nods. "Yes, ma'am, it is."

I gaze into the woods, dark swallowing up what can't be made out. "How much you in for?"

"A few grand."

"Do you have a job?"

"Who's gonna hire me?" he snaps.

His defiant tone makes me bristle, but I do not engage.

Michael is quiet for a while and then he says, "I should've gone your route. Been an officer of the law. That or a teacher."

"What kind of teacher?"

"A history teacher."

I let out a brief smile, recalling the days when we were kids and he carried around a large tattered book about World War II.

Michael says, "Remember when we'd sit around with your grandfather and he'd tell his stories of the Depression?"

My grandfather had been born in the north of

England. When the old man was a boy, his mother shipped him overseas to live with relatives, which didn't work out, so he had to make his own way. The way was unscrupulous and rough, paved with stealing and years of homelessness, but he cleared a path to a small version of the American dream. He secured a wife, a house, and a lifetime job at a paint factory.

"He was a cool dude, your grandpa," Mike says.

I nod. That he was.

"Hey, I'm sorry about your man. I know Carl meant a lot to you. How long is he gone now?"

I don't want to answer because I don't want to talk about my dead husband. "Four months," I finally say.

"How long were you two married?"

I rub my left eye with my knuckle, feeling my throat tighten. "Twenty-two years."

"Whew," Michael says. "That's a long time. Jeez-Louise."

Gloom moves in, circling like a hawk.

"That completely sucks," Michael goes on. "When I heard about it, I felt for you. So unfair, isn't it?"

"Yeah." My husband. His clothes are still hanging in the closet like he's going to come down from heaven and take them to the Goodwill himself because I'm not up to it.

"Tough on you, huh?" Michael says.

I give a quick nod, chase Carl out of my head,

and think about my childhood and my ties to this man sitting on the curb. Michael, after his father beat him in the garage with a jagged piece of wood, lived with my family for a soccer season, when my younger brother played left wing for one of the hapless Lakehurst United teams. Michael and I were both thirteen at the time, and we both agreed soccer was a stupid sport, preferring baseball and street hockey. But we'd been forced to tag along to the games, which were played on the nearby base— the Lakehurst Naval Air Station. Back in those days, there were no soccer fields in the township.

The base was a strange place to play any sport. Located in the north end of the Pine Barrens, colossal gray hangars loomed here, there, like parked spaceships from a science fiction film. The biggest structure, Hangar One, a monstrous old beast, sat steps away from the Hindenburg crash site, or so I had assumed then, for there was no memorial marking it like there is today. As soon as my brother and his team lined up for cleat and shin guard inspection, Michael and I would take off, shouting, racing for the great gray hangar. There we'd roam the wide fields of sand and broken asphalt, searching for pieces of the Hindenburg. Sometimes we lay on the ground, staring into the sky, pretending the zeppelin was sailing through the clouds before it busted up in flames, the debris dropping straight down on us. We'd roll away from the fire bombs, jump, duck, run. Other times we'd just talk about the airship, trying to figure out what had sparked the fire. I had heard it was lightning but Michael insisted it was a bullet or two. "One of them old Pineys was out hunting for deer and looked up, saw the swastika and shouted, 'Shit! The fucking Nazis!' Took it down with their shotgun. Chick-chick, BOOM!"

That must've been in '80 or '81. Lakehurst United was long disbanded, swallowed up by another local league.

"So," Michael says, "you seeing anyone?"

Taken aback and offended, yet amused at the same time, I'm at a loss for words. "Excuse me?" I finally say.

"Well, you know," he drawls, cocking his head, shrugging.

I roll my eyes, forgetting for a moment where I am, and smile faintly. "I can't believe you just asked me that." Michael is a piece of work—you can't give the guy an inch. But it's no excuse to be disrespectful. "My husband just passed, Mike."

Michael doesn't appear to absorb what I said. He grins and goes further: "I'm sure you're sitting around your house, all alone. You must want some company." He winks.

I glare at him, my blood beginning to swirl. This isn't amusing anymore.

Michael wets his lips.

"You should rest." I have to remain pro-fessional.

CIRCLING

Michael laughs. "Come on, Andrea. We go way back. I know you're all bad with your uniform but I remember you in a bikini."

I focus on my breathing which has gone shallow. Yes, we have history. We were friends and sometimes more than friends. Then Carl came into the picture when I was twenty-one and that was it.

"I bet you still look fine in a bikini."

I feel my teeth grit against my tongue. "You should rest."

"Lighten up. Can't a guy give a woman a compliment?"

Lighten up?

"I bet you'd love a warm body in your bed."

I place my hand my hostler.

"Gonna shoot me?"

Do not engage.

Michael is quiet for a minute and when he speaks again, his tone is different. It lacks swagger now. "Andrea, I need a place to stay. Please." He cranes his neck and looks ominously into the dark. "I need protection. They're after me. They're probably watching and you're my only safety. Give me a chance. I can fix things around your house, things Carl used to do."

"Don't bring Carl into this."

"I bet you got a window that isn't shutting properly or maybe your washer ain't working."

"Washer is fine."

Michael frowns. "Well at least Julie will press

100

charges and you'll take me in. Can't get more safe than a jail cell, can ya?"

The front door to the house swings open and Jenkins emerges. He marches across the yard with a stiff gait, then halts a foot away from Michael.

Jenkins says, "Tonight's your lucky night, Mr. McMurran. The lady isn't pressing charges."

Michael's expression immediately turns sour. "What'd you mean? I was bad to her."

My partner's eyebrows squirrel up in puzzlement. "Yes, I know. And she isn't disputing that, but she's not pressing charges either. That's a good thing. For you, at least."

Michael looks at me. "Andie, you gotta help me now. Take me to your house."

Jenkins crosses his arms and grins, gazing at me. "Your house?"

I don't reply.

"Hey, whatever," Jenkins says. "None of my business."

"We used to be together," Michael clarifies.

"Classic," Jenkins says.

I'm so incensed. *Keep it together, Andrea.*

"Time's up," I say, yanking Michael up by the arm and taking the cuffs off.

"Andie, please, honey, you gotta help me out!"

"You're free to go, Mr. McMurran."

"Just for the night," Michael pleads. "So I can sort shit out in my brain. You know, get a plan down."

I shake my head.

"But you gotta take me in. You gotta! I was bad to her!" His voice grows panicked. "And what about my disrespect to Officer Jenkins here?"

"Officer Jenkins is fine."

"But they're coming for me! They're gonna kill me. Please. Take me to jail. Anything. But don't leave me here alone with them."

Michael's voice should tug at my heart. That pleading, I'm-gonna-die-if-you-don't-help-me-now voice. He had a shitty childhood. "Count your lucky stars you and your brother ain't been born in his situation," my grandfather said more than once.

Still, the tug isn't as hard as it had once been. That's the icy, mean truth. Maybe it's because I lost Carl, or I'm dealing with the depression that comes with grief, or the simple fact that Michael hit on me, forgetting his respect. Whatever it is, Michael's problems are the same as they were years ago: *help me write this report or I'm gonna fail out of school; let me borrow money or my dad is gonna kick my ass for taking his cash; save me, rescue me, lend me...*Frankly, I just don't care anymore. I don't. I just don't.

"Come on, Andie." Michael rocks back and forth, shaking, eyes darting. He points to the house. "What if I beat Julie up? What if I knock her around? Will you arrest me then?"

"Why don't you just leave town?" I suggest.

"I got no car and hers is broken down."

"Walk," I bark.

"But you gotta help me! I'm your friend. We go way back. And they're here, circling."

"Circling?" I can't help myself—I start laughing.

"Yeah, they are. It's not funny. They're around the corner, behind the trees, going round and round. I don't fucking know. But I know they're here. Take me home with you. Or just take me in. Put me in lockup. Give me some time to figure shit out."

Jenkins finally seems to catch on. "So this guy's in trouble?"

I don't answer. I walk to the driver's side of the patrol car. Jenkins follows to the passenger side.

"Andrea! Don't leave me! Take me to your house. Just for the night! We're old friends."

I ignore him.

Michael begins to bargain: "Listen. I'm gonna go punch Julie right now. Then you gotta take me in."

"Is this asshole serious?" Jenkins asks.

"Get in the car," I order.

Jenkins hesitates.

"Get in the vehicle!"

He does.

Michael cries out again. "We're old friends! Hell, we had a relationship! Don't you remember? We had a thing!"

I taste blood on my tongue. I shut the door but I can still hear Michael's desperate shouts: "Yo! Come on! Don't leave me!"

Then, "I'm gonna go hit her now!"

Through the windows of the patrol car, I watch as Michael twirls around in a circle, then races across the front yard.

But Michael doesn't go inside. When he reaches the front porch, he snatches up a small flower pot, darts back across the yard and hurls it at my police vehicle. It smashes against the front, pieces of dirt and terracotta skidding across the hood.

"What the hell!" Jenkins roars. "I'm going after him!"

"No!" I shout.

I put the patrol car in forward gear and touch the gas. As I drive away, I catch a glimpse of Michael in the rearview window. The man's hands are up in the air and his face is distorted into a desperate, silent cry, the dark woods behind him. The scene reminds me of the ending of *Platoon,* when they leave the wounded Elias to be killed in the jungle. My husband loved that movie.

"I can't believe you left that joker!" Jenkins cries out. "You shoulda let me at him."

My heart races wildly, my blood flaming, and my hands grip the wheel so tightly, I can feel pain. It is true, I left Michael, and it is something that can come back to bite me. There is no doubt my partner will spill the story—Michael McMurran threw a flower pot at the cruiser and still, Officer Andrea Vogel took off. But getting in trouble isn't what is bothering me. It's the possible outcome: what if one of Michael's phantoms do pop out of the trees and beat him to death? In '99, when Michael had neglected to pay a debt, he got his ass kicked so badly, they had to helicopter his ass up to Jersey Shore Medical Center.

I'm swamped with guilt. Visions of my youth race before my eyes: Michael, nine, knocking on my door to play; Michael, eleven, punching Scott Kaplowitz for calling me a slut; Michael, thirteen, gingerly lifting up his T-shirt, his back covered in horrid bruises and stripes of dried blood.

Shit.

I swing the car around and head back to the house. Jenkins has questions but I order him to close his mouth, that I'm simply having second thoughts about the flower pot.

"Whatever," Jenkins says.

Later, Michael sits solemnly in the car, his hands behind his back, staring ahead, looking relieved.

"Thanks, Andrea," Michael says when we pull into the station.

"No problem," I reply dryly.

Jenkins eyes me suspiciously but I ignore him.

Once Michael is set for the night, safe and sound in a cell, Jenkins shakes his head in disbelief. "I can't believe you went back and got that moron, Andrea. Why'd you help that asshole out? Because you two once had a relationship?" He smirks.

The dig pisses me off. "Watch yourself, Jenkins. I don't like you very much."

He chuckles and shakes his head. "I'll never understand this friggin' place. It's just one big circle around here, isn't it?"

I try to ignore him.

But he keeps going. "Everyone is related, one way or another. By blood or history. And that, in my book, skews everything."

I sneak a glance at skinny Jenkins, secretly marveling at his brief slice of wisdom. The idiot may be right.

In the morning, as I sit at my kitchen table drinking a glass of milk, I know Carl would've gotten a kick out of this story. I can see him now, sitting with me at the table, laughing.

I close my eyes, imagining my husband saying, "Aw, Andie. Old Michael never got over you." I even see him winking at me, as Carl sometimes did. "Poor guy."

Then I open my eyes.

Previously published in Beat to a Pulp.

ELEANOR

Eleanor Webber sat in her TV chair, watching the eleven o'clock news, her eyes fixed on the weatherman. She was having trouble concentrating because the winds lashed at her narrow mobile home, startling her every few minutes and making her look up as if she were waiting for the roof to come off. This was the worst part about living in a place like this—the weather. When it was bad, it made her question her safety and sanity. And it was loud. Great gusts thrashed against the aluminum walls and then moaned, like an angel weeping in hell. She was eighty-four but unlike many of the retirees in the community, her hearing hadn't gone bad. It wasn't great, she couldn't always hear her daughter on the telephone, but that might be because Sharon never spoke up.

Tap-tap-tap.

Eleanor hit the mute button on the TV remote and listened carefully. The winds whipped and whipped at all sides, rapping against the windows and front and back doors, making it impossible to hear if someone was knocking.

It was nothing.

She shifted in her chair, a tan-colored leather

recliner she'd inherited from her husband, Jim, who had never lived in this home. Eleanor had purchased this place on her daughter's insistence. Sharon lived only a ten minute drive away, close enough to come quickly if something were to happen and far enough to keep out of each other's business. She liked her daughter but Eleanor had finally found some independence in life and she didn't want anyone telling her what to do, even her own flesh and blood. Eleanor had a life and she had friends, like Arthur and Ruby Guempel next door. They looked out for each other even though he was a grump and she was a bit touched in the head. There were even some nice widowers in the community but Eleanor was finished with men.

"Why so?" Eleanor's daughter, Sharon, asked recently at a family dinner.

"It's too late to marry now," Eleanor snapped. "I've heard the stories. These old cranks are romantic in the beginning but before you know it, you're washing their shit-stained sheets and wiping their asses. No thank you." She folded her hands on the table and tightened her mouth. Her nineteen-year-old grandson peered up from his smartphone and grinned.

The wind thrashed again, so hard, the glass on her small gray china cabinet rattled. She gazed around her surroundings, looking at the furniture she had acquired over the years. A small gray kitchen table and four chairs, the olive green couch with the wooden lion's feet, the heavy oak coffee table, the large lamps with oversized shades—it seemed too much for the tiny space. Still she kept the place clean, neat, dust-free even though some days, it completely exhausted her.

A commercial for a cologne line aired on TV. Her grandson used those products and he smelled like a dime-store stud. She rolled her eyes and pulled herself out of the recliner, the chair her husband had ruled over for many years. She switched off the TV and turned off the light on the side table. In the kitchen, the fake tiffany lamp glowed, illuminating the room. The china cabinet rattled again and she padded over to it and pressed her hand against the glass to stop the movement. The wind momentarily subsided, followed by a sad low howl.

Something banged against the back door.

Eleanor listened. Was it the wind? The back door was in the laundry area, a fantastic asset—a washer and dryer not in a basement which had been the situation in her former life, in her marital home. Her husband used to bring up the baskets but God forbid he fold and put away the damn clothes.

The rapping came again. It was quicker, stronger, frantic. Someone *was* at her back door.

Eleanor's home bordered a scrub pine forest, filled with turkey vultures and raccoons and hunters, something she was not happy about. "Any

Tom, Dick, and Harry can break in!" she'd said to her daughter, who'd ignored her. The frenzied knocking came once more and she grabbed the baseball bat in the narrow pantry closet. She'd armed the house with three aluminum bats—one underneath the bed, another near the shower, and the third in the pantry closet. Eleanor held it up and crept to the edge of the entry into the laundry area.

Another bang.

Then a whispered call, "Eleanor!"

Eleanor stepped into the laundry area and switched on the porch light. It was Ruby from next door and she had the storm door open, standing between it and the main door. She waved to turn the light out.

"Jesus, Ruby!" Eleanor gasped, placing the bat on top of the washer and beginning to unlatched the three locks. Ruby rushed inside when the last lock had been undone.

"What's the matter?" Eleanor said. "What's wrong?"

Ruby brushed by her with an agitated force. She was a large woman, about seventy-five or so, with thick hands and big feet. In the light of the kitchen, Eleanor saw that Ruby wore a dark parka, navy blue sweat pants and red slippers. Her pink face was flushed and her thin short hair, usually well-kept, now stood up in random points.

"I need help," she cried. "I need help."

"What happened?"

"Arthur. He's hurt."

"Did you call nine-one-one?"

Ruby shook her head. "I can't. I can't."

Eleanor started for the phone on the wall. "I'll do it."

"No!"

"What is wrong with you?"

"We don't need an ambulance."

"Then let me call my daughter."

"No. No. Come over. Just come over."

"I'm in my nightgown."

"Get a robe."

Eleanor shook her head—Ruby was a difficult woman to argue with—and went to the bedroom, grabbing a jacket and slipping her feet into her day shoes. She had to stop for a moment and catch her breath. This happened nowadays. With her aching back, weakening legs, and frailty, Eleanor would give anything to be forty-five again. Was that too much to ask? Not twenty, not thirty, but middle age.

She gathered some strength and returned to her friend. "All right. Let's go."

They headed out the back door. The wind rushed wildly and Eleanor wrapped her tiny arms around herself. She followed Ruby to her back door. Something wasn't right. Why were they using back doors when they always used the front doors?

Eleanor hollered out this question but Ruby swung around and shushed her.

Ruby's mobile home had the same layout as Eleanor's and they entered through her laundry area. The house was completely dark and Ruby whispered to Eleanor, "Promise me you won't scream."

"What?"

Ruby switched on the kitchen light and when Eleanor turned the corner she gasped in horror. Arthur lay on the floor, slouched against the cabinet underneath the sink, half of him covered in blood. It oozed from his neck, staining his light blue pajamas and dripping onto the linoleum. His throat and chin were smeared in it, as were his hands and there was a bloody streak across his left cheek. The nearby white floor cabinets were splashed in red and drops of blood even dotted the counter tops and the thin white blinds over the sink.

"Oh, Jesus! Jesus!" Eleanor cried, her hand going to her chest. Then she saw a small paring knife on the floor smeared with blood, lying in front of the stove. "Did he try to kill himself?" she asked, knowing that might not be the answer. "You have to call the ambulance!"

"He's dead already," Ruby said coldly.

Eleanor looked back at her and then at bloody Arthur. His long wrinkled face had gone gray, his mouth slightly ajar, his eyes open, ghastly and chilling. She approached slowly, careful not to step in the red liquid, moving to the right of the body, then standing in a small section that was blood free. She bent down gingerly—that damned back of hers—and picked up his left wrist, which was still slightly warm. There was no pulse. He was dead.

"Help me," Eleanor ordered and Ruby lifted her up. Their eyes met and Eleanor swallowed. "What happened, Ruby? Jesus, what the hell happened?"

Ruby took a step back and sunk into the yellow kitchen chair. "I don't know."

"We have to call the police. Now." Eleanor's eyes found the telephone on the wall, behind Ruby.

"No, no!" Ruby hollered. "He tried to kill me last night! He tried to smoother me with a pillow!"

Eleanor's legs were shaky and she thought she might collapse. A gust of wind beat at Ruby's home, followed by a malevolent shrill and moan. The windows rattled. Something loud tumbled outside on the road. Eleanor moved across the small kitchen and took a seat across from Ruby, trying to remain calm. "Why didn't you call the police when he tried to smother you?"

"You know how he is. He'd just tell them it was a lie and they'd believe him."

Eleanor glanced at the dead man and then at her neighbor. For several years Ruby had insisted in hushed whispers that her husband smacked her, like she was a disobedient child. Sometimes he grabbed her by the arm and threw her against a wall, she claimed. Ruby told several women at their Red Hat gatherings these tales, sometimes pointing to a faint red mark on her cheek that could have been her rosacea, or a bruise on her arm she could have gotten by knocking against the kitchen counter. Honestly, nobody believed Ruby's accusations, even Eleanor. Ruby tended to be dramatic about life, crying often, exaggerating situations or going berserk over something trivial, like the time she lashed out at Janet Nuccio for cutting her in line at the pastry station. "You did that on purpose! You did!" she'd shouted. "You did!"

Now Ruby sat, sobbing. "Oh, Jesus," she whined. "Just look at him. Look at him."

Eleanor didn't want to and kept her head turned from the gore. What she wanted to do was call the police, but something stopped her. Maybe because the phone was on the wall and Ruby sat in front of it. Maybe because she was frightened by Ruby and this mania. God knows Ruby was bigger and stronger than Eleanor, who was all of one hundred pounds.

"Spit it out, Ruby," Eleanor said. "Tell me what happened."

"Oh, God. What have I done?"

Eleanor reached across the table and took Ruby's fleshy hand. "Go ahead, now. What happened?"

"He, he...oh, God," she said, her voice trembling. She pulled her hand away and covered her wet face. "I'm going to Hell."

"You're not going to Hell. People like you don't go to Hell."

Ruby peered through her fingers. "It's no use. I'm going."

"Ruby, what happened? Were you defending yourself?" It was the first time in their friendship that Eleanor had acknowledged Arthur's alleged abuse.

"I don't—"

Ruby suddenly pounded her fist on the table. "He tried to kill me last night, damn it!"

Eleanor could feel herself becoming weak. Her blood pressure was dropping. Hypotension, a recent age-related development. She sat back and closed her eyes, trying to relax, trying to ignore the dead body which was still losing blood. "I need to sit quietly for a moment," she said.

Ruby sniffled and muttered, "Okay."

When Eleanor felt stronger, she opened her eyes and addressed the situation. "Tell me, Ruby, what happened tonight?"

"He was complaining about the milk," Ruby explained. "He said it had gone sour and it wasn't sour. I just bought it the other day. He said I needed to buy fresh milk and he called me stupid and useless."

Eleanor stared at her. Yes, she'd heard Arthur call Ruby stupid and useless. Several times. That had been confirmed with her own ears. Yet, Ruby had often called Arthur a donkey's ass and mentioned on more than one occasion that he had ruined her life.

"Keep going," Eleanor said, wishing she were young enough to make a run for it. Just get up and race out of the home, run into her own house and call the police. Or maybe she'd run into the dark woods, hiding out in the brush until Ruby gave up and Eleanor could get to the main road and flag someone down for help.

But Eleanor wasn't young. She was eighty-four, frail, completely unable to defend herself. All she had was her mind. All she could do is sit in the chair, in front of this gruesome dead body, and try to find a way out of the situation.

"Tell me, Ruby. Just tell me."

"He threw the milk into the fridge. Threw it! And then slammed the door. I got up and opened the fridge and it had spilled everywhere. Open it. You'll see."

Eleanor used the table to help herself up. She went to the refrigerator, stepping over a stream of blood, and sure enough, the half-gallon was spilled over. She shut the refrigerator door and sat down again, trying not to look at the dead man in the corner.

"Eleanor, I just lost it," Ruby said. "He made a mess that I would have to clean up and it wasn't even my fault and don't forget, he tried to kill me last night! I don't know what got into me." Ruby paused and then said, "I just grabbed the paring knife and jammed it into his neck."

Eleanor stared at her friend of five years. Her neighbor of five years.

The wind thrashed against the walls.

Ruby went on: "I must have hit an artery because the blood just started shooting out in all directions. I stepped away. He pulled the knife out himself, but he fell to the floor and that was it."

"We need to call the police, Ruby."

"No, no. No police. We can't."

"We are."

"No," Ruby begged. "Please. Please. Not yet. Please. Let me think."

Eleanor sighed, tried to keep herself calm.

"You know how it is," Ruby said. "Don't you? When they hit you?"

A sudden rare loyalty came over Eleanor and she pointed her finger at Ruby. "My husband never hit me."

"Oh, come on."

A strong wind swirled around the mobile home, rocking it for a long moment, then lashing at it like the devil's tail. Eleanor lifted her eyes to the ceiling, waiting for the roof to come off.

"We need to get rid of the body," Ruby whispered. "I was thinking. You can call your grandson. He'll come over. He's driving now, right?"

Oh, Christ, Eleanor thought, fear snaking

through her being. *She's gone over the edge.*

"So, call him and he can help us take Arthur out. Nobody will notice in this weather."

"Ruby, our homes are on top of each other."

"We'll go out the back door. We'll get your grandson to carry Arthur through the woods and we'll meet him with the car on the other side. What's the name of that road?"

Eleanor gazed at the grisly dead body, his eyes still open, blue as the sky. She saw the paring knife on the floor. She looked at Ruby and noticed the woman appeared hopeful—no excited—like this were an adventure. Eleanor concluded if she countered Ruby's plan, she could end up like Arthur. Ruby wasn't right in the head. It was best to play along.

"Okay," Eleanor said. "But I don't remember my grandson's number by heart. I have it written down at home. He has one of those smartphones."

"Oh, I bet he's still awake, texting friends. They do that, you know."

Eleanor pushed herself up, her heart pounding. This was her moment to escape. "I'll be right back." She leaned over and squeezed Ruby's hand. "Just stay here."

"I should go with you."

"No, no. Stay here, dear." She patted Ruby's hand.

"Thank you, Eleanor."

Eleanor nodded.

When she got outside, she walked as fast as her trembling legs could take her to the back of her house. The wind was vicious and new rain pecked at her face. She had trouble pulling the storm door open, panic closing in on her, and she began to weep. "Jesus. Jesus." Finally, the wind subsided for a moment and the handle gave way. Three seconds later, she was in her laundry room, slamming the back door shut, latching all three locks. Then she moved towards the kitchen, towards the phone, her hair damp from the rain. Her movements felt slow, like she were in a dream, trying to walk but couldn't. The blackness began to close in on her and her stomach began to grow sick. Her low blood pressure again. She felt faint. Eleanor grabbed her kitchen chair and dropped into it. She closed her eyes and took deep breaths, like her doctor had directed. Soon the blackness began to fade, thank God. The room was quiet except for the knocking of the wind and intermittent pelts of rain against the windows. Eleanor gazed at the telephone on the wall. She willed herself to stand, to go toward it. Her legs were shaky, about to collapse in on her. Yet she moved forward, finally reaching the phone. Her fingers barely worked— they shook, the bones rattling. She picked up the receiver and punched in the numbers 911. She leaned against the wall.

"My neighbor is bleeding. There's a lot of blood. Please come."

The dispatcher asked for her location and Eleanor gave her address, along with Ruby Guempel's. "That's where the body is."

"Body, Mrs. Webber?"

"Just come. I'm not feeling well."

"We will be right there. Stay on the line, Mrs. Webber. Tell me what happened."

Eleanor could feel the blackness closing in once more. She needed to take one of her pills. "I'll be right back," she said, placing the phone on the table. She made it across the kitchen, near the sink, where the pills were kept in a basket. Her hands could hardly get the vial open. Her stomach was growing sicker and sicker and she was sure she was going pass out. But the cap popped open and she was able to get a pill in her mouth. She had left a clean cup on the dish rack and poured water into it from the spout. The pill went down with the drink and she stood against the counter, breathing in and out, waiting for her end which she now swore was coming. *I'm going to die now. This is my time.*

The wind hammered at the outside walls, whistling grim tunes. Eleanor opened her eyes and stared at her reflection in the window. The world was coming back to her. The darkness was drifting away and her head had begun to clear. She was still shaking, her legs quivering, but she was feeling better. The wind moaned and rain blew against the windows but all else was quiet. Eleanor turned around and noticed the phone was off the hook, on the table. She walked over and picked it up again. "Hello?" she said.

"Mrs. Webber?"

"Yes."

"A police officer should be at your house right now. Are you okay?"

"I almost fainted. My blood pressure. It's low."

"Do you need an ambulance?"

"No. I just took my pill."

She heard footsteps on her stairs and sudden beats on her front door. She peered through the window blinds and saw two cop cars parked in front, red and blue lights glittering in the night. "The police officer is here," Eleanor said on the phone. "I'm going to hang up now."

"All right, Mrs. Webber."

Eleanor put the phone in its cradle and walked across her small living room, passing her TV chair and TV, and unlocked the front door. A female officer stood on her porch.

"I'm Officer Vogel, ma'am," the woman called out.

"I'm Eleanor Webber. I phoned you."

"May I enter?"

Eleanor pulled the door open more and the slim officer stepped inside. "Are you feeling all right, Mrs. Webber?"

"Yes, I just needed my pill."

"And you took it?"

"Yes."

"Do you need a doctor?"

"I don't think so."

"Okay. Good. I'll be right back."

Officer Vogel stepped outside and through the front storm door, Eleanor watched the woman confer with another policeman. They bent their heads towards each other, appearing to shout through the rain and wind. Sirens wailed and more police cars pulled up. Two ambulances were coming down the block.

When Officer Vogel returned inside Eleanor's house, Eleanor was sitting down at her kitchen table. The officer pulled off her hat and wiped the rain from her face.

"Would you like a towel?" Eleanor offered.

"No, I'm fine, but thank you," the officer said. "Do you know what occurred next door?"

Eleanor shrugged. "Ruby came over and asked me to see about her husband."

"So you weren't there when the incident occurred?"

"No. I don't know what happened."

Officer Vogel nodded and studied Eleanor, probably searching for cues, trying to figure out if Eleanor was lying. Eleanor thought the officer was a decent-looking woman, in her mid-forties probably. She wore a gold band on her left finger and a little eye makeup.

"If you're up for it," the officer said. "We'd like

you to come down for some questions. A detective on duty can talk to you."

Eleanor swallowed. She'd never in her eighty-four years ever been questioned by a police detective. "All right. I should call my daughter, though."

"Does she live far?"

"Just ten minutes away."

"Give me her name and we'll have someone get her."

Eleanor thought this was a stupid suggestion and suddenly barked at the police officer "You'll scare the living hell out of my daughter, showing up at this time of night! She'll think something happened to her son!"

The officer raised her eyebrows at the defiance. "Okay," she said stiffly. "I'll let you call her from here. How is that?"

"Better. Can I get dressed in decent clothes first?"

"Absolutely."

Eleanor used the table to help herself up and stood for a moment, holding on to the back of the kitchen chair. Red and blue lights splashed against the closed blinds and Eleanor pictured poor Ruby sitting in the back of a police car, her hands cuffed, off to jail. They were going to send her to prison for the rest of her life. Eleanor felt guilty for calling the police but Ruby's idea was ridiculous—Eleanor would get her grandson mixed up in no such thing.

Yet to kill your husband with a paring knife! Christ. The hate must have been brewing for years.

Holding onto the chair for steadiness, Eleanor turned herself around. "I think his mind was going," Eleanor said to the officer, referring to Arthur.

"Who's mind?" Officer Vogel asked.

"Arthur Guempal. He'd been smacking Ruby lately and telling her she was stupid. He tried to smother her last night with a pillow."

The policewoman grimaced. "Why didn't she call us?"

Eleanor gripped the chair. "She wasn't sure she would be believed, I guess. How do you prove it anyway? It's not like you'd have bruises from a pillow."

"We would have looked into it."

Eleanor turned away from the officer and began to walk towards her bedroom.

"Mrs. Webber," Officer Vogel said.

Eleanor stopped, placing her hand against the wall in the hallway. "Yes."

"Make sure you tell the detective about the recent violence. It will help your friend out."

Eleanor nodded. "I will." Then she walked into her bedroom and shut her door, the red and blue lights fluttering against the closed blinds. She wasn't sure the explanation would work, but perhaps they would say this to Ruby during questioning: "Your friend, Eleanor Webber said he was losing his mind lately. Would you agree with that?"

And maybe Ruby would be quick enough to say, "Yes. Yes."

Or maybe not.

It was all Eleanor could do.

She took her jacket off and switched on the bedroom light. She reached in the closet for a blouse and a pair of slacks, and then stopped to listen. The wind had settled down, diminished more or less, and now a steady rain fell. It was as if the devil had come and gone.

She could hear it rush against the roof of her mobile home. It was comforting. Almost.

Previously published in Crime Factory.

ESCAPE

The sound of the motor was faint, like a distant gentle buzz. Leah was sleeping, but as the engine's drone grew louder, it began to wake her, slowly, then quickly, then urgently.

Her eyes flicked open and she sat up. She'd been knocked out on over-the-counter cold medication, but now, with that awful sound of the engine, her heart thrashed inside her body and her stomach clenched. She tried to block out the muffled voices and music from downstairs, and strained to hear the whining of a vehicle coming through the woods, traveling down the dirt road. The clock on the night table read 3:54 a.m. The room was dark.

Leah leapt out of bed and darted across the floor, halting at the closed window. She peered through the curtains and watched as headlights cut through the darkness, flickering between brush and trees. The moon was a slim crescent, barely illuminating the night, and she couldn't see the vehicle but Leah knew it was a truck. The headlights were high.

Oh my God, she concluded with absolute horror. *Brian. How did he find me?*

ESCAPE

* * *

The house where she was sleeping was set at the end of a dirt and gravel road, off a quiet two-lane county highway. Tom Cotter, the owner, tended bar at the restaurant where Leah waited tables. Tom had come across Leah in the parking lot, her tire flat, Leah with that relentless cold, so nervous to go back to her apartment alone—her college roommates were out of town. Tom took pity on the girl and invited her to stay for the night. His brother, Richie, would be home and the house would be warm and safe, so why not stay? One of them would change the tire in the morning.

The evening had not been very quiet. Richie was a big weed smoker, and he and Tom spent the night partying, listening to Phish and the Grateful Dead. After swallowing cold medicine, Leah had said goodnight to the guys, and went upstairs to a guest-room, took off her sneakers and jeans, dropped into the bed. Soon she'd drifted into a medicated slumber, occasionally being woken by a drunken roar.

"Jesus, that's hilarious!" Tom howled from below.

Leah stared through the window, her head still a little spacey, her eyes following the headlights. Perhaps it was a friend of Tom's and her panic was nothing but a puff of smoke.

The truck rolled into view under the slim

moonlight and stopped in front of the house. It was white. Brian owned a white truck.

Leah closed her eyes, her throat tight with dread, and quickly recalled the scene from two weeks earlier: "Baby, I can't live without you. You ripped my heart out!" They'd been standing behind the restaurant, near the dumpsters. Leah told him they were finished—as she had days before—but he said no, they weren't and leaned in to kiss her, and she let him because she was scared, unsure of what to do, because she'd once loved him, or thought she had.

Then she found courage and pushed away.

In response, Brian kneed her between the legs. The blow knocked her to the ground. Horrendous pain stung her vagina and fired through her pelvis.

Immediately, he had dropped down and threw his arms around her. "Oh, God, oh God, what have I done?" he moaned. "I'm so sorry. I love you."

Later, she called the police, got a restraining order, told her boss and co-workers at the restaurant the situation.

Now, the truck's door opened and shut and Leah saw a hulking shadow move across the yard before disappearing under the eaves. *Call the police,* she thought and jumped away from the window, searching for the little bag with her cell phone. Within a minute, she realized she'd left it downstairs, maybe on the kitchen counter. Leah grabbed her jeans and shirt, quickly got dressed, shoved her feet into her sneakers, eyed the window again. There was an overhang she could climb out onto, jump off of, disappear into the woods—if it became necessary.

A loud knocking permeated the house, but no movement from below was made.

She thought of going down to Brian, talking gently to him, maybe promising she'd return, then getting her cell phone from the kitchen counter, ducking into the bathroom to call the police, maybe call her mom, too. But the fear she harbored wouldn't let her. Instead, she stared at the window, pushed the sheer curtains aside, feeling her heart ramming against her rib cage. Another knock echoed, and someone finally answered.

The voices from downstairs were muted and barely audible, overlapped with the gentle beat of music. Leah hoped Tom would say, *No man, she isn't here,* and Brian would go away, but she knew that wouldn't happen. He knew she was there.

Yet, it did happen. The front door shut and through the window, Leah watched her ex make his way to the truck. She let out a deep breath, her shoulders slumped with relief. She even smiled.

But it wasn't over. In a minute, he was crossing the yard again, his gait deliberate with extensive, heavy strides. He held something long. A shotgun.

Leah's mind slid to the edge of absolute panic, her gut sick as hell. Still, she got control, placed her hand on the window and forced herself to wait.

A thunderous burst came from downstairs, followed by a terrible crack—he'd kicked the front door open. "Where's Leah?" Brian howled.

She froze.

An eruption of noise began: Brian called for Leah again, something crashed, and Richie yelled, "Yo, dude, take it easy! This ain't cool!" Another crash—glass breaking. He was knocking things down, probably swinging at objects with his gun.

Get out! her mind ordered.

Leah opened the window wide, ready to escape, but a screen stopped her. There wasn't enough light to see how to unlatch it, so she pushed and shoved and beat at the thin metal, her fists burning from the hits. The frame finally buckled and loosened, and she jerked it free from the casing. But it slid from her trembling hands and tumbled down, knocking against the overhanging roof which covered the wrap-around porch, and fell to the ground.

"Put your fucking phone down!" Leah heard Brian shout.

In a minute, he'd be in the bedroom.

She climbed out onto the slanted overhang, then push the window closed—when Brian got upstairs, she didn't want him noticing her escape route. She stood against the house, then slid along the siding towards the corner. She went carefully, concentrating on each movement so as to not fall, hoping to get around to the side, where it would be safer.

There she would jump, run into the woods, go for help.

"Leah!" Brian's muffled bellow came from inside.

Quietly, she rounded the corner, then slipped into a sitting position and inched her way to the roof's edge, preparing for the jump. A white glow from a downstairs window shone on the grass just below and this is what made Leah hesitate. Brian might see her if she jumped. Could she be fast enough to outrun him if he did? She was in good shape, but she was not a runner, not a sprinter.

When she heard another muffled shout from Brian, she decided it was time, window light or no light. She leapt off the overhang, landing on the ground hard, her ankle turning—pain shooting through her leg. Sucking in her breath, she quickly pulled herself up, scurried across the grass and into the woods, but made no headway because her body became trapped in a tangle of sticker bushes. They stabbed her face and arms fiercely, but she did not cry out. She plucked herself from the trap and turned towards the house again, moving a few paces before stepping behind a slim tree, finding herself on the side of the house, thinking she needed to run towards the highway.

A gunshot went off.

Horror fired through her blood and it took everything in her body to hold it together. Leah searched the dark, seeking in desperate panic where to go, praying that Brian was aiming those shots at the ceiling.

Then there was a noise. An upstairs window slid open. Tom was trying to get out.

"Tom," Leah whispered, waving her hand. "Here."

But Tom didn't see her and seconds later, Leah heard him sob. "Please. Don't!"

Abruptly, the gun discharged—a monstrous blast echoed through the barren night.

Leah's body stiffened, foul bile coming up her throat. She bit her hand to keep from crying. Her throat was tight and she did everything not to whimper, or make any type of sound.

She was just about to run for it, but then she heard Brian outside and quickly ducked down. Leah was still in the woods, huddled in the brush when he marched across the yard, over to the side, right in front of her. He was so close, trudging through the grass, walking into the glow of house light, the shotgun resting on his shoulder like some mad hunter on the prowl. She saw a flash of his face—a crooked nose, big head, longish hair.

In the slim moonlight, Leah saw him pick up the screen.

"Fuck!" he shouted, hurling it into the woods and stomping away. She heard the crunching of rock as he crossed the dirt and gravel driveway, and she heard him climb into his truck, the metal door opening and closing in a loud, shrill whine. The vehicle's headlights blazed and the truck backed up, turned and disappeared down the road, the motor groaning as it went away.

Leah let out a breath—Brian must have assumed she'd run to the highway. She did not budge, remaining in the crouching position, trying to decide what to do: run, or go inside and get her cell phone, call the police.

And Tom and Richie could be alive.

The latter won. She stood and crept along the house, moving deftly, her entire body shaking. She entered through the front door.

The house was silent. The light shone in the kitchen. Leah searched the counters but couldn't find her bag with her cell. She saw the phone on the wall and desperately went for it, but the dial tone was dead—she doubted Brian had cut the lines. Most likely Tom had gotten rid of their landline like everyone else these days.

She walked into the living room, and the misery of it made her cry out: Richie lay beyond the couch, slumped against the wall, shot in the chest. Blood was splashed over his Grateful Dead T-shirt, dripping across the silkscreen picture of the skeleton and rose.

Leah rushed to him and checked a pulse. Nothing.

She began to choke up but restrained her tears, taking the stairs to the bedroom, knowing she'd find Tom. At the doorway, she braced herself and flipped on the light, and there, slumped near the window, was Tom, his eyes open and vacant, his white T-shirt soaked in blood. Shaking, she approached the man, bending down and picking up Tom's wrist, the skin still warm, checking for a pulse. Nothing.

Still, she went through his pockets, looking for his cell phone. Not there.

Leah stood, backed up, and left the room. In the hallway, she began to sob. This was all her fault. If she'd never spoken to Brian, if she'd never gone out with him that first night, if she'd never broken up with him—all of this wouldn't have occurred.

Guilt, horror, hysteria, her head a wreck, not knowing what to do—all of it overwhelmed her as she descended the stairs into the living room. What to do? There was no landline. Her purse was gone. There were no neighbors. She needed Tom or Richie's cell and searched the living room, but could not find a phone. She approached Richie's body, swallowed, forced herself to dig through his pockets, but again, nothing. Where was his cell?

Leah remembered Brian shouting at them to put their phones down. He must've taken them.

The next thought was keys. She could take one of their cars.

She spun around... car keys. Where were the car keys?

A set was on the floor, near the coffee table. She grabbed them and started to leave, but then something moved. Leah swung around, searching the room. It took a moment but she saw what the sound was: Richie had slipped sideways, to the floor, and now lay knocked over like a doll on a shelf.

Leah stepped backwards, told herself to go.

Keys in hand, she shot out of the house towards Tom's old Honda and Richie's Jeep. She wasn't sure which vehicle the keys belong to, so she took a chance on Tom's old Honda, and there was luck. The door opened, she got in, quickly acquainting herself with the car. She started the engine, running the plan in her head: get to the end of the dirt road, get onto the county highway, get to a store with a phone. It would be alright because she could call the police and she would be safe. She would phone her mom up in Carteret. It was going to be okay. She was going to survive.

She backed the car away from the house, put it in forward gear, and began to drive. But she only got about fifty feet before noticing a faint spark of light flashing through the trees. She stepped on the Honda's brakes and stared. The lights glimmered again. He was coming back!

How could she be so stupid? Of course he was returning! He was going to ride up and down this road until he found her, and if she continued to drive, surely she'd run into him on the narrow road and he'd T-bone the car, stopping her for good.

Tears welled in her eyes, but she reined in her

anguish, stopped crying, and tried to think clearly. First, get out of the car.

She jumped out into the raw April night air and listened. The sound of a motor increased and intensified. A cloud sailed across the crescent moon, darkening the surroundings even more. Leah swallowed hard, her mind now becoming clear and sharp. The new plan was to run through the woods towards to the county highway, then flag down a passing car. It was dark and it would be difficult, but possible. She could hide and wait for daylight but if Brian's goal was to hunt her down and kill her, which it probably was, daylight would make her easier to find.

The sound of the motor grew closer and headlights raked through the trees. Leaving the car where it was, she ran and plunged into the forest, making her way through the woods, then turning west, keeping parallel to the dirt road, moving in the direction towards the county highway. The strong scent of earth and pine and oak filled the air.

The truck drew nearer. Leah stopped and ducked down, huffing, catching her breath, watching as the vehicle approached and then passed by, the beams from the headlights moving across the brush and leaves. A part of her prayed it might be another vehicle—a cop, a friend of Richie's—but it was definitely Brian's truck.

He continued on, towards the house, rounding a bend. Leah stood and began to run again, but she tripped, crashing against the earth, tumbling forward into a bush. Twigs scratched at her face and bare arms, her skin aching with fire. In the distance, the truck was still growling, the sound more distant, which meant it was back by the house. She broke away from the branches, untangling herself, and continued to run. Her ankle hurt, the one she'd landed badly on when she jumped, and with this last fall, the pain had worsened. Still, she went on. Her plan became more organized: she'd get to the highway but not run out onto it. Instead, she'd stay in the woods next to the road, continue to run, look for a car to approach, get it to stop.

The rumbling of the truck suddenly groaned louder and louder, the crackling of dirt and rock popping shrilly, signaling the vehicle was traveling slowly and methodically back down the dirt road. Leah stopped running, dropped and cowered down, pressing her body into the ground, the moist smell of the earth filling her nostrils. She waited, her own breath roaring in her ears. Through the leaves, she could see patches of light flashing as the truck rolled by. Diesel fumes wafted through the air, the dirt road grinding under the tires as it passed. Leah closed her eyes and begged God to let the truck keep going. *Please,* she prayed. *Please. Let me live.*

A wind blew, the trees fluttering around her.

But the truck stopped again and she heard the doors open. She was pretty far away from him, but not far enough.

"Leah!" His voice now sounded desperate. "Leah! Come on!"

Terrified he might start hiking through the woods, she thought over and over: *Please don't find me. Please.*

Soon a door slammed, the vehicle went into gear, and the lights faded as the truck grumbled away.

Leah sighed with relief, but didn't leave her spot. She shivered, listening to see if he would return.

He didn't.

Yet it was hard for her to hear, with air growing breezy and the leaves and pine needles clattering against each other. She wished she'd worn a watch. It must be close to five. Sunrise would be coming on.

Leah changed the plan once again, deciding to stay and hide, wait until he was gone. Surely he would give up, especially in daylight with all the people in their cars traveling on the highway—it was a road traveled well in the day, just not the night. As she waited, Leah grew cold and shivered, but she tried to think of calm, simple things— shopping with her friends, the smell of her mother's perfume. But soon her thoughts returned to Brian and that Saturday night they'd met at the party. He'd come to the college to hang out with friends, listen to a band. It was October and chilly, and he'd given her his jacket that smelled like firewood and aftershave. They talked for hours. He called the next day.

Somewhere down the line, it went horribly wrong: he began to accuse her of flirting, cheating, trying to avoid him. He called her vile names—*whore, slut, cunt.* Harassed her with perverse pinches to the waist or the inside of her thighs—twisting her soft skin until she cried. Threw her against a wall. Sat on her face and pressed his ass so hard over her mouth and nose, she couldn't breathe.

The semester at college was almost finished—just three weeks away—and she planned to return home to her mother. "I'm so excited to have you back for the summer, honey!" her mom said over the phone. Leah hadn't told her about Brian's behavior or how he was showing up at work and her place unannounced. When her mom had asked about Brian, Leah said they were taking a break. "Oh, that's good," her mother replied. She was an anxious and intuitive woman, and from the first time she met him, Leah could tell her mother hadn't taken to Brian. "He seems like a nice young man," she'd said later, but her voice was small, stiff.

Now, lying on the ground, Leah forced herself not to think of Brian or the dead people in the house—how her heart ached for them—but of good things again. When she returned home, she planned to transfer to a different college, something close to where she grew up. She'd find a better boyfriend or perhaps she'd take a break from men for a while. She and her mother would go to the movies together, and Leah promised herself she'd help clean out the basement, something her mom had been asking Leah to do for a couple of years.

When the stars had begun to fade, the sky indigo with pre-dawn light, Leah decided to get up. She was cold. Her legs were stiff and her ankle sore, but she was young, and within minutes her muscles were loose. She walked carefully towards the county highway, hoping she wasn't disoriented and going in the wrong direction. She stopped periodically to listen. All was quiet, except for the trees rocking in the wind. He must be gone, she thought, picking up her pace, stepping over thick sticks or small brush that she could now see. Soon she heard the sounds of the periodic car passing on the county road. She was almost there. A lone streetlamp glowed weakly through the trees under the gray morning sky.

She hiked towards the streetlamp. The buzzing of more cars, people on their way to work, filled her with relief. Someone would stop and help.

Then he called her name. It was Brian.

"Leah!"

She turned and saw him emerge from the trees, pointing the shotgun at her.

Leah cried out, swung around, desperately tried

to run to the highway, but it was no good.

He shot her down, two bullets in the back. The girl's knees buckled and she fell, her hands and face hitting the damp underbrush, pain firing through her chest, breathing growing difficult. She didn't die right away, but lay in the wet leaves, her head slightly turned, her eyes fixed on the light of the distant streetlamp as she felt her blood flow out of her body. She heard Brian crying but then all sound stopped.

She thought of her mom.

The streetlamp went dark.

Previously published in Shotgun Honey Present: Both Barrels.

MILK

It's a Saturday evening, June, '92, and Michael waits on the narrow but long concrete porch, a cigarette in his mouth. He's pacing in that edgy, tight manner that defines him, watching for his buddy's El Camino to come rolling down the street. An old song circles in Michael's head, *"Tell it to my heart, tell me I'm the only one..."*

Mike's father appears from the road and trudges across the front yard, his bloated face reddish, grim in the light of the setting sun. He's been at a neighbor's house, shooting the shit, as he says. He's an old-time guy, gruesome, cruel. Michael's grown now, can hit back, but there's a line of respect a young man has for his father.

"You need anything, Pop?" Michael asks as the old man approaches.

"Nope."

Michael nods, takes another pull of his cigarette and watches as his father steps on the porch and passes by. The old man opens the screen door and walks through, but turns around.

"Bring home milk later. We need it for the morning."

"Will do," Michael says.

The old guy nods, growls like he does, then shuts the front door so the air conditioning doesn't get out.

"We're stopping in Toms River," Donald announces as soon as Michael is in the car.

"Why?"

"'Cause I got a bone to pick."

"Fuck," Michael grumbles. He rolls down the window and spits through his teeth. "You and that woman."

Donald rubs his large nose. When he gets older, it will bubble up, go gross like Mike's father. But for now, Donald is at his prime. Twenty-four, pock-marked, and narrow-eyed, he's handsome in a beastly way. It won't get better. He'll marry Tiffany and they'll buy a house and he'll drink on the weekends and after the second kid, she'll start screwing her best friend's husband.

But for now, the night is spectacular, like those summer nights you hang out with a girl. Mike doesn't have a steady girlfriend. He likes them for a little bit and then drops them. Gets bored easily. He had Andrea for a while but the story just depresses him. Why bother thinking about shit that's done and over with? Because on this night, the air is warm with a touch of humidity to let the world know it is June, that summer has arrived. It's rolled out in front of you like life is the day you graduate high school. People in Southern California or Florida don't understand June, Michael thinks. If you live with good weather all year round, June isn't special. It's just another month. But when you live in a seasonal state, you've got to grab June and slow down with it, savor the days, make it last as long as you can.

Mike smiles, impressed with his philosophical thoughts. They're driving down Route 37 now and he closes his eyes, feeling the sweet wind from the open windows blow against his face. When they stop at a traffic light, Michael sits up, lights a cigarette and listens. Crickets sing in the woods.

Tiffany basically lives in her parents' house. It's a bi-level and she rents the bottom section of the structure. There's even a side door and inside she's sprawled out on the mauve-colored couch, her dark curly hair pulled up in a loose bun. Michael finds her ridiculous. She has a large mouth and a mushy body. She's not fat just mushy. But it's her attitude that bugs Mike—lazy, always telling Donald to get her a Diet Coke and whining that she's hot, cold, tired, so on. The place is small, like super small, and before Mike knows it, the couple is arguing about some other dude Tiffany talks to at her job. Mike has to step outside because he hates the fighting. It reminds him of the days his mother still lived in the house with his father. The two of them would go at it but she was never a match for the old guy. He was wicked. Too strong.

Mike lights a cigarette and strolls around back, settling himself in a lounge chair, poolside. He doesn't like to think badly of his father, of all that sadistic punishment he endured. Face near the electric burner on the stove, beatings with belt buckles and tools, countless backhands, kicks in the ass, locked out of the house for days... It isn't worth dredging up old crap. He and his father are at a truce now. Mike is twenty-two. He works at Radio Shack, wears a shirt and tie and black pants several days a week. Some nights he boxes over at that shit gym up in Lakewood. A little Hispanic guy runs the place and calls him Bono because Mike has an Irish last name. Mike has no future in boxing but those guys are cool and he likes blowing off steam.

And there's also this: Mike dreams of going to art school. He's applied to one in Philadelphia. At the moment, he awaits a reply, a possible request for an interview and a chance to show his work. (There isn't much.) Each day he checks the mail, flipping through the white and brown envelopes, hoping to see his letter. It's actually not a long-shot because Mike does have potential. Mr. Thurman, his freaky art teacher from high school, even wrote a recommendation. Mike had to go seek the man out in his dirty classroom and jog his memory with his sketch book and a couple of paintings.

"Remember me? I was your student a few years ago. You said I was good."

"Oh, yes, yes," Mr. Thurman had said, running his hand through his brown beard, staring at one painting of a grayish brown cat resting on a concrete porch. "You've got an eye for the lonely."

The comment was strange. It was just a painting of a scraggly, old cat that used to come around and sit on his porch. Sometimes Mike would give it a bowl of milk. He never thought of it had another meaning. He was just trying to make sure the shadowing was right.

But now Mike knows what Mr. Thurman was saying. My talent might go deeper than just drawing or painting, Mike thinks. I see things, like a poet does. Like Bob Dylan.

Still, it's not good to get worked up about some art school letter. Not tonight. Tonight he draws on his cigarette and studies the fading light in the sky, at the summer orange whisking through the treetops. Mike assumes Donald and Tiffany are talking kindly to each other because he can no longer hear the muffled screams of her big mouth. He can hear kids playing in the street out front. He closes his eyes. Thinks about a girl he'll meet tonight, someone pretty. He's a sucker for pretty. *This is good… this is good…*

* * *

Tiffany doesn't feel like going out so they leave her inside the mini apartment. Ten minutes later, Donald confesses she isn't happy, that she believes Michael is a bad influence on him. They're flying down 37 again, over the Seaside Bridge, onward to the night. Mike doesn't care what Tiffany thinks. Neither does Donald, or at least not right now. Because as soon as they had closed the door to her place, both guys snuck into the pool cabana and did two lines of coke each. Donald is never without blow.

Once they reach the beach town, they go towards the strip, deciding not to park the El Camino on a side street, fearing its beauty will attract the envious and the shiny black car will get keyed. Donald settles on a dirt lot. The teenaged kid taking the money waits as Donald and Mike argue about the ten dollar fee.

"I drove here so you pick this up," Donald says.

"You owe me fucking fifty bucks," Mike says, referring to the poker game they'd be in the other night. "Remember?"

Donald grumbles, leans back against the car seat and digs out a ten from the pocket of his jeans shorts.

When they get out of the car, a gentle sea breeze ruffles Mike's hair. They're only a block away from the boardwalk and the ocean.

"It's gonna be a good night!" Donald cheers as they walk away from the El Camino. "A good night! The ladies are ripe for the picking. Right, my man?"

"Yep!" Mike answers and they high-five each other. But for Mike, there's irony in the slap. Donald will talk this crap all night but he's bound to Tiffany like a marriage vow.

Soon they're on the sidewalk of the strip, cars rolling by, music blasting from the windows, bass thundering. Then they're in the bar, out on the patio, or sand pit thing, whatever it is. It's all fenced in white cast-iron, like a miniature prison yard in Heaven. Big swollen-armed dudes dressed in khaki shorts and white polos stand near the exits like sentries, their expressions lifeless. Girls in heels topple over in the sand. Mike is twitchy, tapping his foot, his eyes darting. Donald and he go to the bathroom and do more blow. All night this goes on, with the tequila, the pretty girls with their fake ugly nails, the beer, the loud *boom boom de da dee* music banging through the speakers. At eleven-thirty, Mike remembers the milk and drums it in his head—*don't forget it, don't forget it.* He lets out a breath and watches as Donald flirts with two girls in black sundresses. Maybe the dresses are dark blue or purple. Mike wants another line of coke but doesn't understand why. He had hesitated earlier in the night, when he stood in the cabana, watching Donald do the first line. Mike isn't a regular user of the drug, just when he's out with Donald or someone else who has the habit. Coke makes the night last longer.

"You all right, dude?" Donald asks.

"Yeah, just bored," Mike answers, lighting a cigarette.

"Bored? The ladies are here and the night is warm!" Donald says, stretching out his long, beefy arms. "We have it all! We're young! Full of masculine vitality!"

"Masculine vitality?"

"Energy. Life! Look at all the women in this place!"

Mike scratches his ear. "Yeah, yeah, I know. But I'm bored."

They leave the bar. They wander down the strip, bump into some guys from Staten Island and argue about who bumped who. Donald takes a punch to the face. Mike hits the other guy twice, hard, like a professional. The dude goes down and for a moment, all step back and stare at the loser splayed on the sidewalk, wondering if he's dead. He moans finally and the enemies nod a sigh of relief at each other, then throw curses and insults out, but go separate ways. Everything is lit in bright lights but the black night hovers over the sky. No stars, no moon. It's like they're on stage, Mike thinks, or in a Caravaggio painting. He's proud of himself again for being so clever. Caravaggio. He recalls learning about the Italian painter from Mr. Thurman. He remembers Mr. Thurman's slide projector and the paintings shining on the white screen—the grayish dirty bodies, the blackness behind them.

Mike and Donald head down the strip. Mr. Thurman's voice pings in Mike's head like a video game. *The subjects were on stage, on stage...*

They end up on the boardwalk, walking through the throng of tourists, shops and game stands flanking them. It's hot, sticky, reeking of sweaty human flesh. The scent of the salty ocean is not strong tonight. Mike stops for a minute and listens for the waves. He can't hear them. It's low tide.

The two walk into a boardwalk bar, do more blow in the bathroom, drink beers, and Mike meets a girl. She's pretty with those long dark eyelashes and red cheeks and he ends up making out with her until her girls pull her away. She writes her number on a napkin but back in the bathroom it drifts out of his hands and ends up on the piss-stained floor.

They do another line.

Drink more beer.

Mike meets another woman, someone with a lean body who reminds him of Andrea, that girl he was with in school. It's the brown hair, the crooked smile. What happened to Andrea? Why did he screw that up? Why did he cheat, lie? Shit.

Another beer.

An angry bouncer throws Mike and Donald out. Last call has come and gone.

They wander around forever, criss-crossing the streets, passing other ghosts who can't find their cars either. Donald is out of blow and he has a connection on Carteret Avenue but Donald says he just wants to go home. He says he misses Tiffany.

"But I can't go see her now," Donald says, picking up his pace. "Not all fucked up like this."

"True, true," Mike says. "You don't wanna do that. She might go and do something wild, like dump your dumb ass."

"Don't start on my girl."

"She'd be doing you a favor."

"I can't live without her."

"You probably could."

They're walking fast now. Donald leans slightly forward as he moves, muttering to himself. "I just wanna get in my bed."

Mike feels bad for Donald because Tiffany cheats on him and he won't see it. Everyone else can. No proof needed. Just that shifty look in her eye.

They keep walking, continuing to search for their vehicle.

Eventually, Mike spots it: the El Camino glowing under a street lamp, windows glistening in the humidity, bulbous tires punching out on the sides, one of the last vehicles in the dirt parking lot.

They get in. Donald is paranoid. Every car that trails them is an undercover cop. Even the old Volkswagen Bug behind them. Donald drives the speed limit, both hands on the steering wheel. "Don't fucking smoke!" he barks at Michael.

"Cops are everywhere. You smoke, they'll think we've been drinking."

"What the hell are you talking about?"

"Don't fucking smoke! Roll up the window!"

Mike switches on the radio but Donald turns it off. "No music. I can't focus."

Mike rolls his eyes and leans back in the seat, staring through the window as they travel over the bridge. The water shimmers under a moon that peeks out from the clouds, in a sky that is clearing up. Then they're on 37. For a stretch it's nothing but fast-food places and strips malls with signs that are dark. Soon it becomes trees and quiet, two lanes. Donald can't calm down. The car behind them is a cop, he says.

"It's not a cop," Mike snaps.

Donald shakes his head, mutters, "We're fucked, we're fucked."

"It's not a cop," Mike says again.

It isn't. It's a pick-up truck. They drive and drive until Donald suddenly guides the El Camino onto the shoulder.

"Jesus, what the hell are you doing?" Mike yells.

"Can't do this." Donald puts the car in park and shuts it off. They sit on the side of the road in the middle of nowhere. The sounds of crickets burst through the vehicle. Mike knows they can't stay. A cop will pull up and Donald will get hit for driving under the influence. Most likely, Mike will be screwed, too, with all that blow in his system.

Mike gets out of the car, goes around the back and over to the driver side. He opens the door and pushes Donald to the side. "Move over, dickhead." Eventually they're back on the road, Mike feeling confident, doing the speed limit but smoking. Screw that.

"You shouldn't smoke," Donald mumbles.

"Shut up."

The highway is dark and Mike knows he has to get Donald back to his house in Lakehurst. Mike is not bringing him home to his father, that's for sure. Antagonizing the old guy with a fucked-up friend is a bad idea. Donald lives with his brother in a rented one-story duplex. Mike won't sleep there. He'll just drop the guy off and take the El Camino back home. Call him in the early afternoon, or maybe later in the week. It'll be good to have a nice vehicle for a bit. His piece of junk only gets AM radio.

They approach town and Mike drives around the first circle, crests the overpass of an old train track, and sees the red and blue lights of the big hangar at the naval base. Then he descends. Stops at the traffic light. He looks at the closed diner to his right and remembers the milk his father wants. There's a 7-Eleven in the distance. He'll stop there on the way home.

Donald has fallen asleep and when they reach his house, the guy won't get out of his car. So Mike does and he stands under a pine tree, staring at the porch light, wondering if Donald's brother is home. He might need help.

"Come on, man," Mike says, holding the passenger door open. "Let's go."

He has to yank Donald by the arm and eventually the big guy becomes awake enough to get out of the El Camino and walk to the front door. Mike shows his friend inside, to his bedroom, and Donald falls on the bed facedown. Mike turns the guy's head to the side so he can breathe.

Back in the El Camino, Mike starts it up and rubs the steering wheel thinking he'd like a ride like this one day. He takes a side street to the 7-Eleven. He's good. He's thinking about his letter. Philadelphia. Art school.

But inside the store, Mike's head is buzzing, ringing and everything under the fluorescent lights seem stark, like he's stepped into an operating room. He realizes he's all whacked out and forces himself to walk normal, grab the gallon of milk, go to the cashier. There's a box radio playing music. *"Come, as you are, as you were..."* Cash slips out of Mike's wallet with ease.

"Want a receipt?" the lady says, sticking the milk in a paper bag.

"No."

She drops it in the bag anyhow.

He gets back into the car and starts it up.

* * *

MILK

To get home Mike should make a left out of the 7-Eleven but there's a cop car rolling down the road and because Mike doesn't want to be a near a cop car, he makes a right on the highway. He's okay. He does the speed limit. Passes the local Lakehurst motel, the main sign in the shape of a neon blimp. He steers the El Camino around a second circle, passes the video store with a porn section in the back. Then a beautiful new restaurant with a gazebo for wedding pictures. Around the circle again. Damn. What's wrong with his brain? Don't go around twice.

Back the other way. The window is open and Mike can feel the summer night. He passes the neon blimp sign. Passes the 7-Eleven. His eyes are sharp but in a warped way. There's a deer crossing over the road and he slows down. He believes he slows down. But he hits the gas harder. What is a deer doing in town?

It's not a deer.

Mike clips it. It flies off to the side and he doesn't know what the hell it is.

He pulls over and jumps out, leaving the door open.

He approaches the object on the ground. It's a man.

The guy is wearing a white sailor suit. A goddamned sailor. From the naval base.

Another car pulls up.

"You all right?" It's an old dude. "What'd you hit?"

Mike thinks he hears the distant sound of sirens. Already?

He peers in the car and sees the brown bag with the milk in it.

"That guy came out of nowhere," the old dude says. "It ain't your fault. Probably got drunk in town and forget to go back to the base."

The sirens grow louder. Mike sees shadows across the street, over by the 7-Eleven. They're walking towards him.

"I think this guy is dead," the old man says glumly, standing over the sailor now. He gingerly leans down and puts his fingers on the man's neck. It's dim and the carnage is barely visible but Mike thinks he sees blood oozing from the sailor's head.

"He is dead," the old man announces.

Mike can feel his brain crashing. He knows he's not right. He knows he's in deep shit.

"It ain't your fault," the old guy says. "I'll vouch for you."

Mike knows it doesn't matter. He's screwed.

He returns to the car. Reaches in the brown bag and grabs the milk by the handle. The bag slips away, drifting onto the car floor.

And Mike takes off running.

* * *

MILK

He races across the two-lane highway, darts behind a gas station, across another road, behind the diner, into the woods. The clouds have cleared and there's a full moon in the sky. Mike moves through the shadows, between thin scrubby pines, sassafras, holly bushes, stepping on pine needles, his bare calves scratching the brush. He's still holding the gallon of milk. Eventually he hears the loud wobbling of the old train approaching. It carries sand and lumber and rocks to Lakewood. He ducks back into the trees, waiting in the moonlight for the first couple of cars to slowly crawl by, then rushes out of the woods and leaps at the side of the caboose, grasping onto the side handle that gleams in the night.

It's not easy to hang on the side with one hand— he's got the milk in the other—but he's done this before as a boy, hanging on the back of a train. In about ten minutes, he's where he needs to be. It's a tricky jump but he pulls it off, flying in the night air, rolling on the side of the ground, the milk slipping out of his hands. The hit hurts, and Mike lays there in the brush, on the ground, staring up at the bright moon. But he has to get going. They're after him. He can hear sirens. So he gets up, finds the milk gallon which has obtained a small dent on the side but is still intact. Home is a fifteen minute walk through woods, skirting the edge of the old gravel pits. It must be a square mile of open nothingness, just dirt. Still, Mike feels someone is behind him. Every step he makes, he hears it. So he stops. Hears nothing. Soon he begins to run. *Run. Run.*

Eventually Michael reaches his house. His father left the door unlocked for him. He goes into the kitchen, puts the milk in the fridge. Then he goes to his bedroom and sits, listening to the silence, the muffled sounds of his father's snores in his room, the ticking of his alarm clock. His head is buzzing again. His nose bothers him. He's congested. He gets up, locks his door. Someone is going to come for him. He goes back to his bed. But he sits for a long time, thinking about his life, his father.

His father could be good. There were days, moments. Michael learned how to play chess from the man. And when his father saw his sketches, he suggested Michael got to art school. "I can even help foot the bill," he'd said.

Michael finally lays his head back. The gentle dawn slips through the chinks in the blinds. He knows he killed somebody. But his eyes are finally heavy and all goes quiet.

They come for him in the bright morning light.

Sure, they trace the El Camino back to Donald but he is reluctant to give up his friend. It is the milk receipt that makes it easy. The cops find the bag in the car and the woman behind the counter simply hands over the video tape. The old man on the side of the road tries to vouch for Michael. He tells them the sailor just walked out of the shadows, onto the highway. Like an apparition. Probably got drunk with the other sailors and passed out somewhere and then woke up.

But the old dude is an old dude and he has liquor on his breath.

Later on, years later, when Michael is out of prison, he'll run into Donald and the big guy will ignore him. Right there in the liquor store. With his stupid fat nose and beer gut. Mike will go to say something but there's no point. Donald has his take: he wasn't driving. "I was passed out in my house," he tells people. "Fucking Michael McMurran dropped me off, took my goddamn El Camino, bought some milk and killed a sailor. Isn't that a kicker? Stupid ass. The car was never the same afterwards, I'll tell ya."

Donald tells this story every so often at weekend parties. It makes a good tale.

Michael's father died of brain cancer when he was in prison.

The letter from Philadelphia did arrive. Right after the accident.

There was a request for an interview.

Previously published in All Due Respect.

DEBBIE, THE HERO

I see that rotten boy who got my fourteen-year-old granddaughter pregnant. I'm just standing here in the 7-Eleven, waiting to pay for my yogurt and coffee, when he walks in with his mother, Melissa, who heads down one aisle, pretending not to see me. I don't know Melissa well but she never bothered me until after the storm, when I became Facebook friends with her. You know the type—always posting positive inspirational quotes like: *God never gives you more than you can handle.* Or, *I love my son! If you love your son and think he's the best thing in your world, share!* Given the present situation, I find these posts obnoxious. Yes, I unfriended her but she's a Facebook user who hasn't discovered the privacy button. Like an addict, I'm drawn to her page, fascinated by her hypocritical posts.

But Melissa isn't my problem. It's her punk kid, Dylan. He's sixteen, cocksure, sporty, aloof. I'm in good shape for being fifty-three—I still have my figure and my looks are decent, but more than that, I'm sure I could swing a bat good and hard, take out his knees.

Dylan leans against the counter like standing is

just too boring for him. He's wearing long black shorts, a Rutgers T-shirt, and black socks that appear ridiculous pulled up to his mid-calf. I scowl at him. He looks away.

"Miss," the cashier asks. I step forward, not taking my eyes off the little shit. He fidgets, scratches his chin, moves away from the counter and disappears down an aisle in search of his mother.

I drive across town, cursing, my hands gripped on the steering wheel, as I head to my bartending job. That boy needs an old-fashioned ass kicking—and I know plenty of guys who will step up—but that will also get me in trouble. Times aren't like they used to be when I was a young woman, when people had codes. Now grown men call the police if they've lost a fist fight.

A billboard catches my eye: *New Jersey. Stronger than the Storm.* The town I live in was hit hard by the hurricane. If you Google Sandy and a picture of a bridge in the water comes up, that's my neck of the woods. I'm only a five minute drive from that spot, where the ocean waves pounded the barrier island, knocked all those old million dollar homes on their sides, and smashed its way into the bay. I don't live on the barrier island but inland, in a regular neighborhood, in a small ranch with one bathroom and a concrete patio in the back. I've been there since 1982, after my husband bought the house as a surprise for me. Lauren, my daughter, was just a baby, my son not conceived yet, and I was rip-roaring angry with Glenn for signing a mortgage behind my back, but what was I to do? In the end it worked out. It's been five years since Joe passed away and now I have the house, and even better, it's paid off.

I work in a small strip mall. The package goods store is in the front and the bar is just beyond it. Customers can come in through the store or they can park their vehicles in the back and enter through a side door. My new boss, Kyle, a young guy with a beard, is already sitting on a stool, drinking coffee. (He makes terrible coffee which is why I stop at the 7-Eleven.) The news is on the TV and they're talking about Sandy. It's been nine months and so many folks are still out of their homes. I say hello to Kyle and he only nods. The writing is on the wall for me. I came with the sale of the bar and clearly, I'm like the old bar stools. Something he wants to get rid of.

"Looking good, Miss Deb." That's Kenny with the scar on his cheek, my first customer of the day. His apprentice, Joel, sits next to him and very quickly, I size the young man up. He's twenty-two, big with knotty hands and strong arms. He reminds me of what I think Wayne looked like when he was young, but I won't think about Wayne right now. What I need to think about is controlling myself, not divulging my private life. And I certainly can't offer Kenny and Joel a thousand dollars to beat the shit out of that punk Dylan.

"You okay, Deb?" Kenny asks and I stare at that deep purple scar on his left cheek. He claims it was a construction accident when he was young, but I don't believe him. Looks like a switchblade accident if you ask me.

"I'm just peachy," I say, pushing a menu in front of him. We don't make food but we order from Luigi's next door. I never eat the stuff. At my age, it's best to stick to yogurt.

Kenny chuckles and looks over the menu. "Peachy, peachy, peachy..." he hums.

The day is long, as always, and when my shifts ends at seven, I sit at the end of the bar, drinking a beer. I do this because the last of the Happy Hour people sometimes forget to tip me and if I sit for twenty minutes or so, they remember and I can make an extra ten or twenty bucks. I don't really need the money but it's an old habit from when I did, and besides, before Lauren and Kiara moved in, I was never in a rush to go home to an empty house. Now that they're there, I don't want to go home at all.

The house is dark when I get in, which means my daughter is out with her boyfriend and my granddaughter is probably home. I turn on the living room light and peer down the dim hallway. A sliver of light glows under the first door. I knock before entering.

Kiara is sitting on the bed, reading a book, big purple headphones on her head. I know those things are expensive, about two hundred dollars. But all the kids have them and my daughter's boyfriend, who I haven't met, said that Kiara should have them too.

Kiara lifts her eyes to me. She's a pale girl with ash-blonde hair and wide cheekbones, a future beauty but not there yet. As a child she was such a nice kid, always drawing, making bracelets with beads, collecting ladybugs. When they came to my house in February, driving down from upstate New York to stay with me for a while, I hadn't seen my granddaughter in a year. She had changed physically—no longer the skinny kid but a young woman with some pretty cute curves. She was still quiet and sweet, but boy did she show her body off. See-through tops. Jeans so tight they rode up into the crack in her ass. I scolded Lauren for buying those slutty things for her but my daughter told me to mind my own damn business, that all the girls dressed this way. After our disagreement, I suddenly remembered my own self in those teenage years—hip huggers dangerously tight, my once-long hair flowing to my butt, braless in halter tops. I blush just thinking about it.

"Did you and your mother talk?" I ask my granddaughter.

Kiara stares at me blankly. "About what?" she asks dully. I hate this habit of hers. She likes to play stupid.

"Take those headphones off," I order.

She rolls her eyes a bit but does what I say.

I put my hands on my hips. "Did you and your mom talk?"

Kiara shrugs and then nods.

"What did she say?"

"I don't know." Kiara looks down at the blue bedspread and picks at it her with fingers. Her nails are fake, the square tips painted black and hot pink.

"She must've said something," I say.

Kiara lifts her eyes to me. "She said I couldn't get an abortion." She shrugs and I see her swallow.

I purse my lips together, feeling heat in my face. I do not agree with my daughter on this issue but there's not much I can do. Kiara is not my child.

This situation has had my stomach in knots, waking me up in the middle of the night, my body in a stiff anger. How did this happen? Why isn't my daughter a better mother? She leaves Kiara alone too much. She buys her things, or the boyfriend buys her things, but she doesn't pay attention to her. Lauren didn't even go to Kiara's art show in April. It was a big deal. Kiara's painting won second place in a county-wide competition.

I step towards my granddaughter and soften my tone. "How are you feeling? Are you sick to your stomach?"

"You mean morning sickness?"

"Yes, that's what I mean."

"I got it."

This breaks my heart. Why is my daughter making Kiara have the baby? I don't know who or what Lauren is listening to these days, and Lord knows she hasn't turned religious because she's still out at the bars at night with her boyfriend, but something unbalanced has wormed itself into that idiot head of hers. How the hell do you let a fourteen-year-old kid have a baby?

"What do you want to do, Kiara?" I ask as gently as I can.

She shrugs again.

I'm getting nowhere. Time to try another tactic. "If your mother left the choice up to you, what would you do?"

Kiara grimaces, like I'd put a plate of spinach in front of her. "I don't want to have a baby."

I nod, not wanting to give away my own views.

"Can I finish my book?" she asks.

"Sure." I watch my granddaughter slide her purple headphones on her head, her strange fake nails fluttering in the light as she locates the page in her book where she left off. It's my cue to leave.

It's a warm, beautiful night so I take my cell phone and sit on my back patio, flipping through the text messages Wayne has sent me over the past few months. He only sends a text every few weeks. When he writes me, I immediately write back and we'll have a conversation for a few minutes. I know he's not married so I have every right to talk to him, but I don't want to push, chase him. But I am disappointed that he only texts. Wayne lives in Virginia, outside of Roanoke, and he was sent up here on a convoy the day before the storm hit. He worked seven days a week, trying to restore power to the area. I worked more night shifts then and after a long day on the job, he and his co-workers would drag themselves into the bar, dark shadows under their eyes, their shoulders slumped. Wayne wasn't a big drinker. A couple of beers and he was off to bed. Later, after things calmed down, he'd get a day off and towards the end of his stay, he slept at my house a few times. He's part native American. His skin is dark, his hair is salt and pepper, his eyes dark. He has a gut and there's heaviness around his neck, but at my age, it's not good to judge on looks like we did when we were younger. It's best to judge the soul and Wayne has a kind soul.

I find the last conversation which occurred on May 24th.

"Hey, darling. You having good weather?"

"Hey, honey," I'd written back. *"Spring is here and the sun is shining."*

"That's good, darling. Don't spend the whole day in that dark hole you work at."

"I'm not. I have the day off."

"Very nice. Enjoy."

"You too."

I put the phone on my glass patio table and sit back, breathing in the cool night air. Lightning bugs float over my small yard, glowing like yellow stars. It was kind of the gods to send me Wayne, even if he was with me for a short time. Like a young woman, I find myself dreaming of him, fantasizing about moving to Virginia. Simple images pop up in my mind: ironing a shirt for Wayne, cooking up lasagna for an evening dinner like I did when he was here. Wayne said he'd never tasted such fantastic lasagna. I explained it was the egg in the ricotta cheese. "The egg makes all the difference."

After I'd said this, Wayne put his fork down and took my hand, bringing it to his lips for a kiss.

Lauren comes home about midnight, liquor wafting off her breath.

"You gotta take Kiara to a gynecologist," I say. "She needs to be looked at."

"I know," Lauren says, dropping into her father's old recliner.

"Do you have insurance for her?"

"I don't have insurance myself," my daughter snaps. "What makes you think she does?"

I close my mouth and breathe through my nose before speaking again. "There's a clinic in Howell."

Lauren stares at the television. "She's not getting an abortion."

"The clinic doesn't just give abortions."

"That's where you're going and I told you it's not happening. She's my kid and I decide what happens to her."

I can't hold back anymore. "You're making the wrong choice. She's just a child."

"Abortion is murder."

There's no use arguing with Lauren. When she gets something in her mind, you're just wasting energy and I'm too tired tonight to waste my energy.

After barely sleeping, I give up about six-thirty and get up for the day. I'm standing in front of my living room window, drinking a cup of coffee and watching the birds in my Bradford Pear tree when an old brown sedan cruises by but suddenly halts in front of my driveway. The birds fly away in one swoop. The windows of the car are rolled down and I notice Dylan is in the front passenger seat. The other boys push at Dylan, laughing, and soon Dylan is too. Then the car speeds off. My heart is battering and my blood feels thick. I watch the birds return to the tree. They flutter from limb to limb, to the wooden feeder which hangs on a branch, then to the ground, up again, whistling with happiness.

I imagine taking a baseball bat to Dylan's handsome face. Bash, blood, teeth.

About an hour later, my daughter still fast asleep in her old bedroom, Kiara pads into the living room and sits on the couch. She's skipped school again, something she's been doing once or twice a week since she found out she was pregnant. I don't bug her about it. It's the end of the year and she hasn't failed anything yet. She'll make it out of the eighth grade.

Kiara turns on the television with the remote and I wonder if she saw the boys in the car. Her room faces the street. I offer to make her eggs but she says no.

"How about a glass of milk?" During my two pregnancies, I craved milk.

She stretches out on the couch, resting her head on a burgundy throw pillow, ignoring my question.

"You sick, honey?"

Kiara gives me a short nod.

"A little food will make it feel better."

She shrugs.

"How about I get you some toast?"

"Okay."

I go into the kitchen, put bread in the toaster and pour a glass of milk. When I bring her the breakfast, she is fast asleep. I put the plate and glass on the coffee table and drape a blanket over her. Right now, she has three weeks of school left. The kids are going to the very end of June because they were out for two weeks in November on account of the storm—most of the county didn't have electricity. She's two months gone and at the moment, the pregnancy isn't noticeable. But in September, she'll be showing. My granddaughter will be a freshman in high school and she'll be wearing maternity clothes.

The sun is shining and the air is warm. I have the day off, so I decide to spend a few hours at the beach. I'm aware that at my age that sitting in the sun isn't good for my skin, but at this point, it doesn't seem like the wrinkles at the corner of my eyes or the small lines around my lips are irreversible, so why bother? And I know I may be risking skin cancer but I use strong skin block. Truthfully, I'm tired of hearing about what is good for you and what is bad. You can't spend life hiding from everything that is dangerous.

The drive over the bridge is a sight to see—the houses along the ocean that had once blocked the view were washed away during the breach and now you can see clear out to the water. I drive south, towards Lavallette, passing so much destruction—houses on their sides, houses half standing, houses with debris in the front lawn. Later, as I get farther south, I pass Normandy Beach, where a gas explosion occurred and set off a fire which burned an entire neighborhood. The charred remains are blocked off by a chain-link fence.

Lavallette is in pretty good shape and I take my spot on the sand, far from other lone beach goers. This is the best time to come to the beach—the beginning of June. There are no lifeguards and the tourists, which we call Bennies, haven't arrived yet. So it's just us locals, sitting in our chairs, reading our books. I'll probably come here a few more times before I stop coming all together in July and August. I also like the beach in September, when the Bennies have gone, before the October cold sets in.

The ocean is deep blue and vast before my eyes. Using my cell phone, I snap a picture of it and plan to send it to Wayne later because cell service is spotty near the ocean.

My feet sink into the sand as I watch four teenagers rush towards the water. I smile thinking of the days when I skipped school for a day at the ocean. Those days were so thrilling, so fantastic. Everyone was young. Everyone was happy. Standing in the sea, looking out to the horizon, it felt like my life was like the Atlantic before my eyes—wide, unending, superb. Now I watch as the teenagers fight the waves, laughing, screaming, but pushing themselves farther into the cold sea. The water is rough, wave after wave crashing, and I see there is no lifeguard to help them if they get in trouble. Suddenly I think of Kiara and my mood grows dark. She'll never know what it's like to rush into the ocean without a care in the world, to be naïve, to think the world is a wonderful place. Whatever happens to her, abortion, miscarriage, or having the baby, she will always be a hundred years older than these kids throwing themselves against the ocean waves.

Fury overwhelms me and I cut my day short. Soon I am in my car, passing the broken houses, trying to control myself. I punch the steering wheel. Something has to be done. Someone has to pay. I picture myself waiting for Dylan in the morning when he comes out to catch his ride to school. I see myself charging forward, knocking him to the ground with my bat and giving him a good kick to the stomach. In school I was in a couple of fights and I'd done that same move to this girl who had called me a slut.

When I get home, Lauren's car is gone. Kiara is in her room, asleep. I sit at my computer and log onto Facebook. I look up Melissa and see she has a new message up:

Never reply when you are angry.

Never make a promise when you are happy.

Never make a decision when you are sad.

"And never let your son get an eighth-grade child pregnant," I mutter. What an idiot. I scroll through her list of friends and find Dylan. I click his name. Just as I suspected—too dumb to secure his page. All of his comments are visible.

But there's nothing telling, nothing mentioning my granddaughter, just bullshit chit chat with lots of *fuck, asshole, mother fucker* shit.

My daughter is still not home by six. She works for her boyfriend doing secretarial crap for his landscaping business. They went to high school together and although they didn't know each other well then, they are in love now. Lauren tells me he's wonderful and he sounds like he's okay but it's the beginning of a relationship, so he's on his game right now.

I order a pizza for dinner. Kiara eats three slices. She says she's starving and I'm happy she eats. But in the middle of the night I hear her vomiting. After the last of it seems done, I get out of bed and stand outside the bathroom. Just as I'm about to knock, I hear her crying. I turn away, telling myself she needs privacy but truthfully I don't know what to say.

Kiara goes to school the next morning and I head out for my shift. Kenny, Joel, and two Hispanic men—Kenny's day laborers—sit at the bar, eating Luigi's meatball sandwiches. I turn on a soccer game for the Hispanic men. They thank me and I smile.

It's pretty quiet so I lean against the back bar, examining my nails, which are chipped and broken.

In the old days I would have lit up a cigarette but there is no smoking in public places anymore and besides, I quit after Glenn died.

I need someone's opinion about Kiara's situation. I used to have a couple of close girlfriends but they moved to Florida and I haven't spoken to them for a while. Now I have no one to ask. I could call Wayne but I don't know how he feels about the subject of abortion and frankly, I don't want to know. If he's against it, it might change my mind about him. If he senses I'm not against it, it may change his mind about me.

While I think about asking Kenny and Joel for their opinion, I recall my own teenage years in the mid-seventies. Legal abortion was fairly new and it seemed accepted by everyone, or maybe that's how I remember it. One neighbor was thirty-seven years old, a mother of three kids, when she had an abortion. "I don't need any more children" was her reasoning. My father was appalled but my mother secretly told me she understood and didn't blame her one bit.

"I want to ask you guys something," I finally say to Kenny and Joel, framing my story as hypothetical. "Suppose you had a daughter who was thirteen or fourteen, and a neighborhood boy got her pregnant."

Joel looks straight at me but Kenny just takes a bite out of his sandwich.

"It's not anyone I know," I say, quickly trying to

cover up my true motives. "I was just watching something on TV and it bothered me, you know? How things get under your skin?" My lip begins to curl but I force my mouth straight.

Joel seems to accept the explanation. Kenny bites into his sandwich again.

"Well," Joel says. "I'd kick the kid's ass."

With a mouthful, Kenny shakes his head and holds his finger up to wait until he's swallowed. Finally he says, "You can't do that anymore. Assault charges against a minor has a pretty tough penalty."

Joel shrugs and nods. "Yeah."

Something I pretty much know. I push on to the next issue. "So what do you do with the pregnant kid? If she's really young, like thirteen or fourteen. Do you think you think she should have an abortion or have the baby?"

This time, Kenny shrugs and mutters, "Don't know."

Joel goes off on a tangent: "What I say is that the fathers have no say in whether a girl gets an abortion or not. They get no rights in the legal system, not even when the kid is born. My buddy hasn't seen his daughter in two years because the mother told the courts he beat her up and I know he didn't lay a hand on her."

I eyeball Kenny. He's in his mid-forties and he's had a difficult life, so I'm expecting some type of wise empathetic answer. But what he says stuns and makes my brain crack.

"Abortion is murder. And it would be her own fucking fault for spreading her legs. Girls need to know to keep 'em closed and not grow up to be skanks."

My gut tightens and my hands shake. I swallow and nod, move slowly away from them. I spend the rest of the time standing next to the Hispanic guys, watching the soccer game, chewing on my nails until they're bit down so low, I've drawn blood.

Still, I think about what Kenny said, about why Kiara had sex with Dylan. I'm sure she was lonely, being the new girl. I'm sure, after school, as she walked home, Dylan and his friends drove by, saw her, and made conversation. He's a good-looking kid. I bet she welcomed his attention. I bet he came knocking one afternoon and she let him in. It's easy to think he raped her but I don't think that was it. I even asked my daughter if that had been the case but Lauren said Kiara said no, he didn't force himself on her. Truthfully, I was once in those shoes. When I was a sophomore in high school, a boy told me he'd be my boyfriend if he I let him go all the way. And when my mother was gone, I'd let him in my bedroom. It must have happened at least three times. I was lucky, though. I didn't get pregnant. I bet Dylan was in my house a few times.

I want to call my son, Ryan. He's a sensible person and he'd probably side with me, but like Wayne, I'm not sure. Still, he's a wonderful young man—twenty-eight years old, married two years to a sweet woman, working for a company outside of Pittsburg, just put a down payment on a cute colonial with the life insurance money his father left him, money that sat in a bank account for five years! Lauren had her share spent in months. New car. Cruise to the Caribbean with her then-boyfriend. Ryan was always responsible. He never gave me a hard time as a teenager or even as an adult. He and his wife drive eight hours to spend time with me on my birthday and holidays. I know it's tough on them and I know he'd rather be with his wife's fun, happy family in Pittsburg, but my son is dutiful. I want to tell him he doesn't always have to be the saint in life. That he should do something irresponsible, a little unsafe. He should lie and tell me he can't come for Christmas this year because his wife's mother is sick.

Later after work, I sit at my computer and I check Facebook again, looking at Melissa's page.

It takes two to tango.

My stomach lurches, knowing this is code for the situation. So why hasn't she come by my house, asking for confirmation? If my son had gotten a girl pregnant when he was sixteen, I'd be over at the girl's house, demanding to speak to the parents, wanting to know what was going to happen. I search Melissa's page, looking for clues into her psyche, something about how she thinks about. I find nothing. I try to remember back to the those first nights after the storm, when we had no electricity, when we all stood together in front of Ray Hudson's fire pit, drinking beers and talking about the storm. It was spooky, those nights, listening to Ray tell us about the rumors that looters were coming in by boat, robbing folks. My house is just eight blocks from the Metedconk, an inlet into the bay and I spent those freezing nights alone, wearing three pairs of sweat pants, four long sleeved shirts, a bat, and a cleaver near my bed.

My house did come through fine. No trees down, no broken windows, nothing at all. I remember I thanked my dead husband a hundred times because I knew he was looking out for me. When he died, he had left the kids a fifty thousand dollar life insurance policy for them to split, and another one for me: a hundred and fifty thousand. After paying off the funeral expenses, the house, Ryan's school loans, a credit card of Lauren's and buying myself new Toyota Corolla, I was left with about seventy-five. My children don't know about this extra money. Glenn left it for me because he knew I needed it to survive. I live off my bartending salary but just as Glenn had predicted when he was dying, I wouldn't be able to tend bar forever. After Christmas, Kyle replaced my former night shifts with a young lady named Jessica. She's blonde, nice, and easy on the eyes. The men like her. Not only does she have some night shifts, but she now works my old Tuesday day shift. I'm aware that Kyle is trying to push me out. Who wants to look at an aging female bartender when there are so many young ladies out there?

Still, I need to focus on the immediate problem. I get off Facebook and do some research.

Kiara is lucky to be in New Jersey. Parental consent for an abortion is not mandatory, like in other states. The next morning, I put a call into Dr. Salzmann, my gynecologist, and he confirms this. He also gives me the number for a clinic in Cherry Hill, which is down by Philadelphia. They don't do abortions in the hospital, only clinics, he says. He talks to me in that quiet voice of his, giving advice, telling me what will happen to her, and offers words that I can say to my granddaughter after the procedure is done.

I thank him and make the appointment.

A couple of days before I am scheduled to take my granddaughter to the clinic, Lauren finds me on the patio and tells me Kiara has decided to give the baby up for adoption.

"So many couples out there want a child."

"Where's Kiara?" I ask.

Lauren rolls her eyes. "In her room. Where else?"

181

My breath becomes shallow and I take a moment to get a hold of myself, to play along. "Then you need to take her to the doctor. She'll need pre-natal pills."

"Yeah, I know," Lauren says, sitting down. "It will just have to wait another month. My insurance kicks in then."

I look out into my yard. The grass is lush and green as it is always in June. By August it will be brown and burnt. I'm not good at keeping up my yard. Glenn did the outside. I close my eyes and think about Lauren and where I went wrong. Sure, she didn't get everything she wanted but she never starved. Glenn and I didn't have the best marriage but it wasn't the worst. We had money troubles, we argued, we flirted with others, we were distant to each other at times.

Lauren gets up and leaves me to myself, and I let out a deep breath, enough to scare away the rabbit that had snuck under the fence.

The evening before the appointment, when my daughter is out with her boyfriend, I go into Kiara's room and tell her not to eat anything for twelve hours.

"Why?"

"Because you can't have anything in your stomach when they do the procedure."

"What procedure?"

Again, the stupid act.

"You've got a one o'clock appointment for an abortion tomorrow," I say. "You don't have to decide tonight or in the morning, if you don't want to do this, we can forget this whole thing. But if you want to have the procedure, after your mom leaves for work, I will take you to the clinic. I just want you to have a choice. I'll pay for it." The abortion will cost almost six hundred dollars.

My granddaughter picks at her fake nails. I brace myself for whatever answer she gives me and moment later, she speaks, still looking at her hand. "I want an abortion."

"Okay," I say, shutting her door.

It is a long day of waiting. Forms are filled out, magazines are read. The room is dingy and the receptionists sit behind glass. I wonder if it is bullet proof. There are mostly teenagers and young women who sit in the hard plastic seats and they chatter, talk on the phone, twirl their hair, examine their nails. Some sit with what I think are their mothers and others sit with friends. They are white, Hispanic, black. My granddaughter sits silently with the purple headphones on her ears. I don't try to make conversation. Eventually the door opens and her name is called. She returns twenty minutes later and hands her iPod and headphones off to me. I won't see her for another hour and a half. I know the procedure doesn't take that long but she must be counseled, examined, and she must have an ultrasound that she can choose to look at or not. I know in other states they are forced to look at the fetus and I thank God that we are not there.

When she comes out, she is dressed and looks the same. I put my hand on her shoulder but she doesn't react. I tell her she must be hungry and she nods. "Can you take me for pizza?" she asks.

"Sure," I say.

Again, we don't speak. We stop at a pizza parlor and order a pie and still we don't speak. It's not until we are on our way home that she says something.

"They put me in a room and there was this book called *Emotions*," she says. "I looked inside and all these women wrote stuff to their babies. They said they were sorry they couldn't have them. They said they felt terrible. Some said that relatives, like their grandmas, will take care of them in Heaven."

My throat grows tight. I swallow and keep my eyes on the road. "Did you write anything?" I say, sneaking a glance at her.

Kiara shrugs. "I don't feel anything," she says quietly. "I didn't feel anything."

We're quiet for a while and I realize her headphones are not on. I grab my chance to speak: "I'll tell your mom you had a miscarriage and that I took you to the hospital. Tell her it was very painful and then tell her you don't want to talk about it."

"Okay," Kiara says.

"But, if you want to tell her the truth, that is your choice. I'm just giving you another option."

"I like your option."

"That's fine." A traffic light comes up and I stop on the red. I take the opportunity to say one more thing: "I know you don't feel anything right now but you may later on in life." I recall what Doctor Salzmann said. "Don't beat yourself up about it if you do feel something. You're fourteen, Kiara. You're too young to have a baby. You made a mistake. One out of three women will have an abortion in their lives."

I look at her and see her face brighten sadly. "Really?"

"Yes," I say. "You're not alone."

"Did you have an abortion?"

I didn't, but I remember my neighbor. I remember a friend in high school had an abortion. "No," I say to my granddaughter. "But I knew women who did."

"My mom wanted me to help a couple who can't have children."

My mouth clenches and it takes a second for me to answer. "You're too young to have that type of responsibility. Simple as that."

She doesn't respond, so I add more of what I want to say: "And even later, if you do feel bad about this, you remember that you were only fourteen and your grandmother made the decision for you. You blame this on me. Don't go through life blaming yourself." I pause and then say, "Because I'm the one who pushed you into this."

"Okay." She puts her purple headphones on and we are done talking.

In the end, I tell the lie to my daughter about the phantom miscarriage. She doesn't believe me for a second. Within hours, they are gone, moved in with that boyfriend of my daughter's, down in Forked River. This may sound cold, but I'm glad. I don't want this responsibility. I'm sorry I didn't try harder to be closer to my granddaughter but hopefully, deep in her heart, if she needs my help, she knows where I am.

But there's nothing I can do about that now. All I can do is go to work, get my days in at the beach, and ignore people I don't want to know. I vow to stop checking Melissa's Facebook page and decide not to beat the shit out of her shitty son. I keep my contact with Kenny with the scar down to a minimum. He asks me one day if I'm okay. "You seem quiet lately."

I tell him I'm tired. That old excuse usually works well whether it's the truth or not.

* * *

On the Fourth of July, Wayne sends me a text.

"Hey, darling. Happy Fourth!"

"Happy Fourth to you too!"

"I'm going to give you a call tomorrow. How's noon?"

The breath in my lungs stops for a moment. I bite my lip to stop the smile. My son Ryan and his wife are with me and we are sitting on my patio, having just finished eating burgers and corn cooked on the barbeque.

"Noon would be great."

"Good. I want to come up. I have a week vacation. September sound all right?"

"Yes. Of course."

"Good. Talk details tomorrow. Bye now."

"Bye."

I look up at my son who is staring at me. "Who's that?"

"Nobody."

Later, after my son and his wife have gone to bed, I remember my picture of the blue ocean and send it to Wayne. He doesn't respond and disappointment floods through me. I don't trust things yet. I just don't.

Finally, about an hour later, his reply text comes in.

"Looks like just what I need."

I don't write back. I just lay my head back on my pillow, dreaming of him. I hope he comes in September. I hope there's a chance for us, a chance for me. But even if his trip never happens, at least I'll have a few weeks wishing for it.

IT'S HARD TO BE A
SAINT IN THE CITY

This isn't the city. It's Lakehurst, or Manchester Township, same difference, where the Hindenburg crashed, the cover of the Zeppelin albums. Those things peak your interest for about thirty seconds when you drive through the area. Springsteen music still hums in the diner, in people's cars, but he never comes here. It's the middle of nowhere New Jersey, nothing but scrub pines, empty roads. You want a city? New York, sixty miles north. Philly, forty miles southwest.

But back in '91, Heather Sullivan is going to the city: London, England! And because Eddie and Phil are unsuccessful locating weed at an ex-girlfriend's house, because there's an altercation with the Wortreich brothers, leaving Ed with a nasty pain in his shoulder from smacking into the outside brick wall of a video store, Phil suggests they hit Wawa to brighten up the night. Then he smirks. Because two things are going to happen at Wawa: one, Phil will hook up with Carol in the back room; two, Eddie will get to talk to Heather.

Now these are the days when Wawa isn't the cooperate giant it is now, when the convenience

189

stores are small, when two women working alone deep into the night is no big deal. Anyhow, just drop your mind into the old days, back when Eddie Callahan is on the skids. He's okay now. Runs the meetings. But every alcoholic has one of these—not the shocking, sad, crazy tales. Those are easy to reveal. No, this is more complicated. It's a moment, a possible turning point, a brief window when things could have gone another way. Maybe. Sometimes these things are bigger in our memory than they were at the time. You be the judge.

So here we are, one cool September night, and Eddie doesn't know why he's agreed to hang out with Phil. His head is mush and he looks like shit: eyes swollen, the rims red, hungover from a three-day extravaganza of cocaine and alcohol, upsetting his father for sure. Eddie's dad is a good man, a parent who hasn't given up yet, although he has threatened to throw his son out of the house when he turns twenty-four, just months away. It's sad the way he says it—calmly on Sunday afternoons, when Eddie sits in the backyard smoking a cigarette, staring at his step-mother's flower garden. "I have to, son. For your own good." His voice shakes when speaks and it crushes Eddie's heart.

The convenience store is slightly tucked back off the main road, surrounded by woods. It's set in a strip mall with two banks, a travel agency, a bakery, a drug store, and a pizza parlor. At this time of night everything is shut but Wawa and the pizza joint. There are three senior citizen retirement neighborhoods nearby, filled with elderly people who lived through the Depression and World War II, but they don't come out at night. Only a ghostly quiet hovers over the parking lot.

Inside the store, a box radio sits behind the deli case and a Jackson Browne song murmurs softly. Phil and Eddie—jeans, jean jackets, grungy white sneakers—make their way to the back, finding Carol at the desk in a tiny smoky office. She's on the phone and when she sees them, she grins. Carol is Heather's aunt or something. She's a shift-manager, in her late-thirties, slim, cool, a former homecoming queen candidate, still hot, but she's got a head full of problems. You know the type.

Carol hangs up the phone, leans back in the desk chair, and stares at Phil. "Sweetie, where've you been all my life?"

Phil laughs. "Looking for you, baby."

Eddie turns and walks away, closing the door behind him.

He scans the store and notices Heather behind the deli case. Eddie doesn't know what to do—go outside or talk to her, but he loves talking to her, so he takes a breath and walks across the store, stopping when he reaches the deli case. She's hunched over, wiping tiny pieces of turkey and ham from the edges of the glass. After a moment, she straightens up and faces him, tossing the dirty rag onto the back counter.

"You know..." he chokes out.

"What?" she snips.

Her angry tone shocks him but he soldiers on: "Two girls shouldn't be in this place alone at night. It's kind of dangerous."

She slams the deli case door shut.

He holds up his hands in surrender, then leans against the counter, near the sink, and winces from the pain in his shoulder. Jimmy Wortreich is such a dick. What was he piss angry about? Did Eddie owe him money? Eddie owed everyone money.

He takes out a pack of cigarettes. "Can I smoke?"

Heather walks past him, opens a bottom cabinet door and pulls out a box of sugar packets. "Sure," she snaps, dropping the box on the coffee station counter.

Eddie nods, lights up, and gazes across the dingy store. Remember in high school when he sat next to Heather at a party in the woods? She looked like she'd rather be in a thousand other places. He had his dad's car parked only feet away. "Come on," he'd said to her. "I'll take you to the Boardwalk."

"Ha!" she laughed, then smiled. "You think Jesse would let you get away with that?"

Jesse was her boyfriend at the time. Camo jacket. Chew in his mouth. Not a bad guy except he had what Eddie wanted. "Hell, I'll kick Jesse's ass," Eddie had said, throwing punches in the air.

Now she isn't smiling. "You don't have to hang

around, Ed," she says, shoving sugar packets into black holders of the coffee station. "I don't need your protection. The knives are sharp here."

Eddie blows out cigarette smoke and chuckles. She cracks him up. But he doesn't want her mad at him and he doesn't want to bullshit. He wants to know details. He wants to ask her out. If he had a drink, maybe he'd have some balls. But he's an idiot when he drinks.

"Carol says you're going to London in a couple of months."

Heather nods.

"What are you going to do there?" He takes another drag on his smoke. His lungs ache.

She closes the sugar packet box, returns it to the bottom cabinet, and kicks the door shut. "Stay," she replies.

"Stay?"

She puts her hands on her hips and faces him. "Yeah. Get away from that shit." She flicks her head towards the closed office door. "And this place." She throws her hands up in the air, implying everything around them.

Eddie taps his cigarette ash in the sink, tries not to take it personal. Heather been nice in school, although because she was a year below him, he never knew her super well. He just wanted to. Forever he'd wanted to.

The bell on the door chimes and a man walks in. Heather jogs to the register on the other side of the store and rings up a pack of cigarettes. When she returns, she picks up the rag again.

"Are you gonna marry someone in London and stay?" Eddie asks dryly, jealous. He puts his smoke out in a black ashtray on the counter. "Is that the plan?"

Heather narrows her eyes. "Don't be so sexist. I don't need to marry to anyone." She starts to wipe down the counters at the coffee station. Then she sighs. "But marrying someone will make it easier to stay."

Eddie chuckles and shakes his head, trying hard not to look her up and down. She's slim but not skinny, fair-skinned, decent chest, cute in a Meg Ryan way. Surely she'd be hot as hell in a tight dress. But that's not her style. Jeans, Converse, pissy attitude, that's her style. He adores it. "Well," he says. "Getting married shouldn't be a problem for you."

She ignores this comment. "You know, they let Canadians and Australians stay in England for two years. But Americans get six months."

He's hopeful. "So you're coming back in six months?"

"I'm getting married. Remember?"

Eddie laughs.

"Why do we only get to stay for six months?" she asks again, but it's more of a question to nobody. "Seems strange, don't you think?"

Eddie shrugs. "Must be all that Revolutionary War business."

"Ha!" Heather points at him. "You're probably right." She wipes the counters once more.

"How come you're not moving to New York?" he asks. "It's a lot closer."

"I don't want to get shot."

He grins.

"Everyone goes to New York. I wanna do something different."

"Can I come with you?" he asks.

She stops for a quick moment, frowns at him, and then continues wiping the counters.

"Yeah, I know." Eddie laughs but it suddenly turns into a cough. He leans over the sink to steady himself.

She quickly gets him a cup of water from the soda machine. "You should see a doctor."

"I should do a lot of things," he says grimly, coughing again, gripping the edge of the counter.

When he finishes, he turns to her, feeling flushed. "So I'm making an impression, huh?" He sniffs and wipes his nose.

"Are you sure you're okay?"

Eddie sniffs again. "It's nothing. So what are you gonna do in London? Do you have a job or something?"

Heather sighs and stares at him for a long moment. "Well, I'm not working around food, that's for fucking sure. In fact, I'm going to find a real job, something that doesn't make me smell like ham and turkey."

Eddie smiles. "Like what?"

She shrugs. She says she isn't sure, just that she wants to do something interesting and that she wants to wear something nice every day. "Maybe I'll work for a solicitor. That means lawyer in American." She winks.

Eddie nods. "I can see you dressed up in heels and a skirt. A city girl."

"Yeah?"

"Yeah."

She goes on to describe London, explaining that she'd been there for a semester in college, something Eddie already knew. "I just love it there. Tons of pubs and nightclubs. If you like music, it's an awesome place to be."

Eddie briefly closes his eyes, imagining himself walking along the city streets, everyone looking like Boy George or Joe Strummer.

Then the cough returns. He hacks for an entire minute like an old man.

"Are you okay?" she says.

He shakes his head. "It's nothing. Too much partying, that's all." He wipes his mouth, turns away from the sink, and rubs his face.

A Bruce Springsteen song comes on the radio.

Heather swings around and spins the dial, changing the station.

"Don't like Springsteen?" Eddie asks.

She huffs. "I'm one wrong turn from being a character in his songs."

He chuckles and nods knowingly. "Yeah, I'm familiar with that."

Heather smiles gently.

Just then, the office door bangs open and Phil appears with a wicked smirk on his face. "Let's jet," he calls to Eddie.

Eddie doesn't move. It's too soon. He doesn't want to leave. He doesn't want to go anywhere. "Heather," he says.

She looks at him.

What if he goes home, sleeps off this hangover, gets up, has breakfast with his father, and calls her? He'll pick her up in his dad's car, take her somewhere nice, that new Italian place on Route 37, then to the Boardwalk for a bit. He can do this. He can straighten up for her, for himself. She likes him. He knows it. We all know it. But she's not going to waste her time on an alcoholic cokehead, so he has to get it together. She'd be good in his life. Maybe she wouldn't go to London. Maybe they'd get married. It's possible. It is. Take this road, Eddie. Take it.

But he can't. He wants a drink first.

"If I don't see you," Eddie says, touching that pained shoulder of his, "have a good time in old Londontown. And give me a ring when you get back."

"I'm not coming back."

The last words hurt terribly as if he's been knocked sideways against that brick wall again. He becomes depressed. He gets in the car with Phil, rests his head back, watching the dark roads sail by. Later, they're at Carol's house, and the three of them drink her booze and do her cocaine.

Heather does return from London but Eddie is living in some hole in Asbury, drinking himself stupid. When she sees his father, she asks after him. Then, there's a car accident on Route 70, about a quarter mile from where the Hindenburg crashed. She and her little Honda are crushed by the tractor-trailer. Heather is twenty-seven. It takes an entire year for Eddie to hear about it.

Funny how the people you peg for dying young come through. Eddie is in his mid-forties now, solidly on his way to old age. No cancer. No aches. No nothing. He's got no wife, no kids, just tries to help young men like he once was, men missing all the good stuff that you get when you're twenty-three, twenty-four.

There's this too: he wishes Heather were alive. He doesn't dwell on it, it doesn't wreck his day, and he never has trouble with women, but it'd be cool if Heather were around. Maybe she'd be divorced, separated, something like that. He'd ask her out this time.

Previously published in Trouble in the Heartland.

KICK

Erica steered her car along Mantoloking Road, approaching the cross street, a funeral parlor on her left, a realtor office on her right. The stink was still in her nose, snaking off her dirty clothes—the sour smell of a house that had been flooded.

The water was gone now. When she'd pulled into the driveway earlier in the day, her little bungalow was still standing, appearing nothing like the wreckage she was told it would be. For a moment there'd been hope.

Then she got out of her vehicle and noticed dozens of clam shells strewn across her small yard. She saw a neighbor's lawn decoration—a wooden sign that read, *Fisherman Lives Here*—resting in a bush. Still, she had hope.

The front door was busted. *Did the wind do that?* But the thought left her mind when she pushed the door open and encountered an overpowering rotten, vile stench. Her hand went to her nose. The floor moved when she stepped inside, sagging slightly under her footfalls. Even though the water had receded, its mean damage was done. The house was finished.

In addition, her new LED television that hung on

the wall was gone. A fancy new lamp purchased at Pier One was missing too.

"Looters," Mark, the neighbor next door, explained, standing on his porch, drinking a can of Bud Light, staring at the bay. He offered her one and seemed relieved when she declined. It looked like only a few beers were left, and it was only eleven a.m.

"They came in trucks," he explained, lighting a cigarette. "Night, day, who knows?" Mark had stayed through the storm, had taken refuge on his second floor. "I tried looking out for everyone's homes, but I musta been asleep when they hit your house." He drew on his smoke, shrugged. "They were here quick. Like flies to shit."

The day was bright, sunny, only a slight cold breeze off the water. Erica looked around, saw the boats toppled over in the canals, noticed patio furniture tipped on their sides, but all appeared serene.

Mark seemed to read her mind. "All those houses are done. They all took on water."

So now, with an hour left of daylight, her clothes dirty from carrying out ruined furniture to the end of her driveway, Erica drove, heading towards her sister's house. "You stay here as long as you want," her sister had said. She had wanted Erica to wait to check on her house, wait until she could get someone to watch the kids, wait until her husband was off of work. Erica tried to wait, sitting around her sister's house without electricity, listening to her nieces play Monopoly, bickering about who was going to buy Boardwalk. Erica was lucky to have somewhere to go. She reminded herself this.

Now she approached the Yield sign, across from the Italian restaurant she'd never been in. She stopped her vehicle, let traffic pass, spaced out for a moment.

The honking began right away. A long heavy drone, followed by three short beeps, then another long drone. Impatient.

Her poor house. The yellow walls were warped. The new carpet, not even paid off yet, destroyed. The fifth mortgage payment, due in a few days. Was she supposed to pay it? Erica stared at the restaurant, the empty parking lot. The honking was a faraway clatter, like a distant firehouse alarm. And then the noise was close, mean blasts jarring in her ears. Her house, gone. The honking, there. Erica suddenly snapped, anger flicking in her chest. She put the car in park, got out of the vehicle, walked back to the van behind her, faced the culprit—a thirtyish-year-old man with dark hair and silver-rimmed glasses.

"What's your problem?" she demanded, rage eating her at her insides.

"You stupid idiot!" he barked. "Get the fuck in your car and go!"

"Fuck you!"

His face was red, enflamed like a rash, and he opened the door to the van.

Fury shot through her blood, took over her muscles, knocked out all reason in her brain. She lifted up her right leg, the leg that could still kick a soccer ball from the midfield line into the goal, and pressed it on the door. With one push, she slammed it against the van. The door bounced back at her and she kicked it again, this time shut. The driver was shocked, enraged, and he began to scream: "You fucking bitch! You almost took my hand off!"

"Good!" she barked, turning and storming back to her car. She got in her vehicle, put it in drive, sped forward. Her heart was racing, her hands tight on the wheel, her breaths short. She peered into the rearview mirror and saw that the man was behind her, a phone to his ear. Probably calling the cops.

He trailed her across town, through several intersections. Most of the traffic lights were out, and getting around was difficult. Still, he kept on her.

Eventually they hit a spot where a cop was directing traffic. The guy in the van pulled over. Erica drove on, watching in her mirror as the guy got out, walked across the street, and approached the cop.

It took a long time for Erica to calm down, to get her heartbeat to normal, to get her bones to stop rattling. When she arrived in Freehold, her sister was waiting for her. Even though the storm had knocked out their power, her sister's husband had a generator hooked up, a fire burning in the fireplace, and there was a pot of sauce cooking on the gas stove.

Erica told her sister the story of kicking the van, then of the guy stopping the policeman. "That's all I need. To be arrested."

Her sister laughed, handed her a glass of wine. "I'm sure the cops can't wait to deal with that one."

Erica smiled, nodded. Then she told her sister the story of her house, of the looters, of the clam shells on her front yard. She finished the wine quickly and began to weep.

Previously published in Literary Orphans.

FINN'S MISSING SISTER

Bobby Kovacki, five-foot-ten, muscular, right upper bicep inked in a skull tattoo, left bicep inked with a spider, exited the gym, holding the door for a tiny teenaged blonde who smiled kindly, but her friendliness did not move him. He was thirty-seven, too old for teenagers, and besides, he had a woman, a married one at that—taking on a second, a possible jailbait, was not what he needed now. He was grumpy, sweaty, and gross, irritated because Moronhead, five-foot-five, too much tanning, had harassed his workout with bullshit chatter: "Hey, Bobby—check out the girl on the treadmill. I'd liked to nail that." Bobby didn't even remember Moronhead's real name, although Moronhead used Bobby's name generously.

The gym was a short car drive from the local convenience store, a place Bobby liked to hit after his workout to grab a blue Gatorade and any other items he might need, like some sliced turkey for a sandwich or a half-gallon of low-fat milk for his protein shake. As he walked toward the store, he waved to Pete Finn, who usually could be found sitting in his van at this time of day, chain-smoking and drinking coffee. Finn was a gangly tall man with a pot belly, a head of untamed brown hair, and a thick beard streaked with gray. He was a roofer and in Bobby's book that was all one needed to know to about the guy. Today, though, Finn wasn't in his van but outside it, standing, chain-smoking and drinking coffee. It was a windy March day and Finn's hair blew wildly.

"Yo, Bobby!" he called.

Bobby nodded, pretending not to hear Finn, and continued on his path into the store. Finn's second job was selling pot and many of his connections were made in front of the convenience store. Were the cops onto him? Yeah, how could they not be? Any doughnut who's ever watched an episode of *CSI* or *Law and Order* could call that one. So why was Finn permitted to park his van in the same spot every day and carry on his side business? Bobby couldn't tell you. Bobby and Finn and a few of the cops went way back to high school and sometimes, in dead-end towns like this, cops let people like Finn slide for no reason. Finn was a likable guy, and he'd been a likable guy in high school, a guy with an alcoholic mother and absent father, a guy who was at all the parties in the woods, a guy who always had the pot. New Jersey was a funny place and in these parts—parts that were not of the Passaic County Soprano-land, parts that were not even on Springsteen's "Thunder Road" radar, parts that were forgotten wasteland, the Pine Barrens, where the mob dumped the bodies and the Boulevards were empty—in these parts, guys like Finn kept the locals stoned and stupid, which gave the cops people to trail and something to do. At least, that was Bobby's take on it all.

"Yo!" Finn called again when Bobby emerged from the store. "Come here."

Bobby let out a short breath. Despite Finn's past and present popularity, the guy, just like Moronhead, annoyed the shit out of him.

"What's up?" Bobby asked when he reached him.

"Dude," Finn said quietly, his eyes twittering back and forth. "Yeah, how ya doing?"

Bobby nodded impatiently. "Fine. What's up?"

Finn took a long drag of his smoke and exhaled. "My sister, you know, Janine?"

Bobby nodded again. Yeah, he knew Janine. Yeah, years ago, and more recently, he'd slept with her. Now she was in her thirties, still good-looking, but used, used, used.

Finn moved closer. This act repulsed Bobby. Finn's breath was violent, stinking like a neglected dog's.

"Yeah," Finn whispered. "My sister's gone. Missing. Vanished."

Bobby held his face stone stiff, but the act was hard because Finn's breath was horrific and the story was downright outlandish—everyone knew Janine had a penchant for bottom feeders. She was probably staked out in some lowlife's house, strung out on who-knows-what, giving it up for the drugs. Bobby didn't say this, though. Instead, he went straight for the advice: "Report it, Finn. That's what the cops are for."

Finn nodded as if this was the first time he'd heard or even thought of the idea. But then he ran his grubby hands through his ragged pothead-dealer-roofer hair. "So, you know Wicky?" He meant Tom Wicky, straight-edge cop depending on which angle you were looking from. Bobby, Finn, and Wicky had all spent time in woodshop together.

"Yeah, I know Wicky."

"He knows where she is," Finn hissed.

Bobby didn't believe this for a second.

"So the cops won't work, you know, Bobby?"

"Yeah, man, I guess not."

"No," Finn said seriously. "Not at all."

Bobby rubbed his eyes. He was tired. The night before he'd worked at job number one as an overnight security guard for an industrial park.

"Can you help me, bro? Can you make some calls?" Finn asked.

Calls? Who the hell was he going to call?

"You know people, right, Bobby?"

Sensing the best course of action was to agree to the plan, Bobby said, sure, no problem and he'd get back to him as soon as possible.

Finn dropped his cigarette, stepped on it, and lit

another one. "Thanks, dude. 'Cause I know something's not right. I feel it here." And with that, Finn punched his heart.

"Hey. Can I come over?" It was Penny, the woman he always took a call from, no matter what was happening.

"Yeah. I just gotta shower."

Penny, a beautiful brunette, a nice girl, mother of two boys, curvy from her pregnancies but not fat, was married to a shithead who made a lot of money doing something Bobby had forgotten but, lucky for Bobby, left his wife alone too much. The shithead had had a mistress for a couple of years and, after getting caught, did the standard apologizing, begging for forgiveness, and laying out the promises as long as a toilet roll. The stock honeymoon period followed, until eventually, things positioned themselves back into the same routine with a new mistress. Instead of throwing him out, though, Penny took up with Bobby. Bobby wanted her to leave the shithead, but he'd never really asked. He'd hinted, but she hinted back—divorce was bad for kids, she said. Made them too sad. Made them fall into drugs. Made them losers.

"So this guy I know," Bobby said to Penny. "His sister's missing." Penny was getting dressed and he was in the bed, watching her. Their time together, as it always was, left him satisfied but wistful, needing more. He wanted her to stay longer; he wanted to feel her breath on his chest as she laid her head in the crook of his neck. But her boys had to be retrieved from the school bus by three-thirty and Penny was a responsible mother. Once, Bobby'd seen Penny and her family in the Home Depot. Her shithead husband was typical—tall, handsome, neatly groomed. But her kids were what got Bobby. They weren't the rugrats that he and his brother had been. These boys were clean-cut, appearing to be the studious kind but happy, not the type that were too dorky, victims of bullies. They seemed to be boys who could do complicated division problems but at the same time find their way through the woods. Bobby couldn't blame Penny for staying with her husband. Her boys wouldn't have a chance if they moved into Bobby's run-down house. Although deep in his heart he hoped otherwise.

"What do you mean, his sister's missing?" Penny asked. "Is she a teenager?"

Bobby said no. "She's my age. She has a son, a kid about fifteen, I think." Bobby remembered the scandal. Janine had gotten knocked up by Joe Brodbeck, who had been engaged to someone else. Stuff like that was common.

"Anyway, Finn wants me to look for her."

"Who?"

"Finn, Janine's brother."

Penny pulled on her boots. "Bobby Kovacki, Private Detective."

He grinned at her. "Come here."

She slid into bed and kissed him.

"Stay a little longer," he whispered.

She shook her head.

Later, as he prepared for his second job—he was a door person at Donovan's Pub—he thought about his affair with Penny. Bobby was not afraid of her husband. Yeah, the man was taller than Bobby, but without question, Bobby could put him down in two hits. What he worried about was the shithead putting an ax to their romance. These days, Bobby didn't think he could live without Penny.

Penny didn't work even though she had a college degree in Art History. She was smart but what Bobby loved about her was the way she looked at things—at all sorts of angles. When he told her he felt guilty for solely inheriting his dad's house after he'd passed from cancer, that maybe he should sell the place and split the difference with his brother, she shushed him and kissed his lips. "Your father was just looking out for you. You were there during his illness. You took care of him. Where was your brother?"

His brother was in Florida or was it Texas? He had a drug problem. Had done some time. He didn't even make it up for their father's funeral. He was a loser.

Still, Bobby felt bad about his brother. When they were teenagers, their mother left them and Bobby's brother hadn't coped well. Bobby hadn't been supportive in those years, hadn't taken him under his wing, hadn't looked after him. He was too busy screwing around with girls, hanging out with guys like Finn, telling his little brother to fuck off and get a life.

"Lighten up on yourself," Penny had said. "You were a kid, too."

Bobby appreciated these reassurances, but he was careful not to reveal too much. He figured some of Penny's attraction to him was his mystique, his closed self. Mostly their relationship worked because he listened to her—her thoughts, her dreams, her desires—while he kept himself locked up, an enigma that fascinated her.

About midnight, as a light fog rolled in, Finn pulled his van into Donovan's parking lot. Bobby watched his gangly former classmate get out of the vehicle and approach the bar. Donovan charged a cover on Friday and Saturday nights to pay for the bands. Bobby liked to stand outside and collect the money because the music was too loud and Bobby's hearing was sensitive these days. The shrill wailing of the singers and raucous winding of guitars sliced through his ears liked miniature cleavers. Even on chilly damp nights like this one, it was better to be outside.

"Yo, man, thought I'd find you here," Finn said when he reached Bobby. A cigarette hung from his lips. "Did you get any info on Janine?"

Bobby shook his head, explaining he'd made a couple of calls, but nothing had come of it—all of it a lie—but Finn bought it, nodding gravely. Bobby felt guilty and offered to let him into the bar for free.

"No, dude," Finn mumbled. "I got my weed." He drew on his cigarette, pulling it away with his weathered roofer's fingers. He was quiet for a moment before speaking again: "Wicky did something to her. I just know it."

Bobby grew irritated again. He hated weekends because Penny was unavailable. He hated feeling anxious and unsure and sad. And now, he had to deal with Finn and his missing sister shit. "Finn, I hate to say this to you, but she's probably off on a bender. You know how she is."

Finn closed his eyes and opened them again. "Her kid is real scared, Bobby. He's been staying with his dad, Joe, and you know Joe don't give a fuck's sake about my sister, but the kid is scared. The boy got the feeling in his heart, too." Finn touched his chest. "It ain't like Janine to be gone for so long."

Bobby asked, "How long?"

"A fucking week, dude. A fucking entire week."

213

A quiet shudder went through Bobby. A week was a long time and it reminded him of his own mother's disappearance. Nobody heard a thing from her until she called seven days later. Bobby remembered his father hanging up the phone, announcing quietly, "She ain't returning boys. Sorry."

"You know my sister," Finn continued. "It just ain't like her. Sure, she likes to party, but she's a standup to her kid. Always home on Sunday night when Joe brings the boy home. It ain't like her."

A couple approached the bar and Bobby checked their IDs, taking five dollars from each of them. The guy moaned about having to pay to get inside.

Bobby said, "I'm sure there are cheaper options out there."

The young woman frowned, embarrassed.

The guy said, "Yeah, whatever."

After they went inside, Finn pressed the issue again. "You know Janine was fooling around with Wicky."

Bobby didn't know, although it wasn't a surprise. Just like Bobby and Janine, Wicky and Janine had messed around years ago in school, at outdoor parties in the woods. Wicky always had a nice girlfriend, the type of girl who had curfews and strict rules. Janine was a different type of girl, and, after a few beers or hits off a bong, both Wicky and Janine would disappear into the woods, nobody ever spilling the beans to the girlfriend until Janine got fed up with being the side screw. Wicky lost two girlfriends because of Janine's jealousy and mouth.

Finn said, "You know how Wicky is, man."

Bobby hated all this twenty-year-old high school bullshit which hovered around like a bad stink. He hated that he was still hanging around the area, running into people he wished would hit the pavement for good. He'd tried and tried again to leave New Jersey—first taking off for Seattle but that was in '96, two years after Cobain was dead and, honestly, even if the guy and grunge had hung around, that Northwest grim weather would've still driven him away as it eventually did. Next, he headed down to Arizona, but all that dry heat kicked his butt, so he tried the Carolinas, but all the Southern niceness got under his skin. He eventually settled in Boston with a girl, but two years later, he got the call from his dad and packed up for Jersey. He didn't want to marry that girl anyway.

He only wanted to marry Penny.

"I think Janine was hoping Wicky'd leave his wife for her," Finn said. "But Wicky ain't the type to leave his wife."

About this, Bobby agreed wholeheartedly. "Yeah." People like Wicky, with two kids, a dog, and a four-bedroom house, don't leave their wives for women like Janine.

Bobby guessed Janine pressed Wicky to leave his marriage, he said no, and she threatened to tell his wife. Knowing Janine, she'd have evidence: cell phone records, e-mails, and texts. Possibly photos. Back in high school, she had one of her friends take a picture of her and Wicky kissing and presented this proof to the first girlfriend. The second one didn't need a photograph. And, now that he'd thought about it, it was possible Wicky had done something to Janine. Years ago, Wicky possessed a piss-vile temper. Once, he put a sophomore's kid hand under the circular saw in woodshop—Bobby and another guy had pulled the kid from harm's way. Another time, Wicky beat the shit out of Finn—broke a couple of ribs and put him in the hospital—all of this violence for stupid infractions. So sure, Bobby thought now, it was possible Wicky had done something to Janine.

Still, Finn, just call the cops. It wasn't like this was 1933 and this snitching would buy him a bullet in the head. The local cops weren't that powerful or devious. They'd arrest Wicky and no harm would come to Finn, except maybe his weed business might go on hiatus. What was the great big fear?

"I don't know, dude," Finn said. "I guess I'll head out." He turned and shuffled away, the orange end of his cigarette glowing, a gentle misty fog swallowing the rest of him as he walked back to his van.

* * *

The following night, Bobby awoke about four in the morning, thinking about Janine, about how she was years ago after Wicky dropped her and Bobby took over. He had seen them walking through the dark woods, searching for a place to be together, she leading. "Careful, Bobby. Fallen tree branch."

When he told Penny the mystery of Janine was still bothering him, she nodded solemnly. He explained a little more about Janine: that she was a partier—a big drug user—but always returned home Sunday nights for her son.

Penny suddenly smirked.

"What?" Bobby said.

She rolled her eyes and laughed. "This woman sounds like she's worth finding. A real class act. Kind of like your brother, huh?"

Bobby swallowed hard. Her cruelty stabbed through him.

She gently hit him in the arm. "Just kidding, baby."

Still, joke or no joke, he wanted to hurt her back. "I have some interest in this, you know," he said a moment later. "I used to fuck Janine."

Penny winced at the vulgarity, language he refrained from using around her. "Oh, you did, huh?" she whispered.

He nodded. "She gave an awesome blowjob."

A shadow crossed Penny's pretty face.

Bobby asked her to leave. "I have to go into work early tonight, so I gotta get ready." It was the first time he'd ever kicked her out.

"Okay," she said quietly.

During the week, he worked from four to midnight at his night guard job. He drove around the industrial park, then sat idle for a while, and drove around again, keeping an eye on female swing shift/graveyard workers as they walked to and from their cars. The job was boring but he occupied his time with the radio or his iPhone, reading the internet. Bobby liked working nights instead of days. He liked driving home in the dark, the roads clear and quiet. He liked knowing he could stay up until three and sleep until eleven, hit the gym, and wait for Penny. This routine suited him.

But during the last few days, his sleep had been disturbed. He kept waking up, thinking of Penny, hearing that mocking laugh. Something was wrong. He loved her—he was sure of that—but did he like her? It was an odd question, yet it plagued him as he lay in bed, staring into the dark, the room silent. And then when he'd drift off, fleeting visions of Janine would pop in his head: Janine talking, Janine kissing him, Janine twirling around a fire.

After his shift on Thursday at one in the morning, Bobby drove to Baskro Lake.

Baskro was an old titanium mining pit that had been turned into a reservoir years ago. During his teens, this was the spot where Bobby and his friends built fires and drank and did drugs and had sex and got into fist fights. It was a great place to hang—far away from the menacing police or complaining neighbors. Baskro was only reached by a few dirt roads.

Baskro was a peculiar lake—wading offshore for a few yards, the water would only reach the knees. But suddenly, like a bizarre trick, the bottom would drop off, and a swimmer might as well be in the middle of the Atlantic. The lake was extremely deep and over the years, several kids and teenagers had drowned. Explanations for their deaths popped up as urban myths and people told them like ghost stories: discarded exotic animals like alligators or sharks had bitten and eaten the swimmers; the water had a strange undertow which pulled the swimmers to its center, tiring them out, and swallowing them whole; Baskro was cursed with the specters of dead miners; the pressure of the deepness acted as suction, yanking its victims into death. Even though each story made some sense and spooked him, Bobby never believed one. His take on it was more simple: the kids panicked when the bottom dropped off, and because it was night and because they couldn't swim, they died.

The drive out to the lake was eerie, just as it always had been. When his truck's headlights illuminated the dirt road and peripheral brush, opossums and deer stood still, their eyes glowing red. Scrub pines and oaks drooped over the trail, branches swinging in the wind. When Bobby reached the dark water, he parked the truck and got out at the old spot, a place littered with beer cans, overturned plastic buckets used as seats, cigarette butts, and off to the side, condom wrappers. Soon, he returned to his truck and drove further down to a more secluded spot, an area he and Janine used to hide out in. Bobby was never really fond of Janine, but like he'd told Penny, her sexual skills were very good, and at the time, that was all Bobby was really looking for in a girl. Years later, after his father had died, there'd been another stint with Janine, but that'd been in his house and lasted only a couple of weeks.

Bobby turned off the truck and opened the window. The lapping of the water and moving of the trees lulled him to sleep.

At dawn, he woke and stepped out of the truck. He walked near the shore, peering into the dark blue water, then stopped and glanced around. The lake was very large, long, and beautiful, oddly undeveloped and natural-looking, undisturbed. But Baskro Lake was anything but natural. It was considered a hazardous waste site, monitored by the DEP. There would never be any development—

lake houses, cabins, jet ski launches. It would remain forever as it was now, a vision of serenity and purity, but deep down, polluted and deadly. Bobby bent down and ran his hand through the water—the temperature was icy. He stood up and wandered some more along the shore, at one point coming upon a wet red shirt in the sand. He picked it up with a stick and threw it into the brush next to a brown beer bottle.

The next two nights, he worked the door at the bar. Finn did not appear, and during the day, after going to the gym, Bobby saw him at the convenience store, in his van, smoking and drinking coffee, barely nodding his head to Bobby when he passed by. Penny came every day that week, but strangely, his desire for her seemed washed up. "Are you okay, baby?" she asked on Wednesday.

"Just tired is all," he said. There was truth in this because each night after his shift in the industrial park, he drove out to Baskro and parked in the same secluded spot, remaining until dawn. He didn't have a concrete explanation for why he followed this routine, but an odd sense of loyalty to Janine had something to do with it. On Friday and Saturday night, Bobby also went out to Baskro, yet came upon some teenagers. He quickly waved and turned the truck around. On Sunday, the teenagers were gone, and he was able to resume his habit.

About four in the morning, he heard the sound of a car.

It was pitch black and quiet, a moonless and windless night. The lake had been quiet and the trees silent until the sound of the distant motor. Bobby waited in his truck, the lights off, his hand on the ignition, ready to turn and speed away. The distant motor went on for what seemed forever, but by the glow of his truck's digital clock, only a minute and a half passed. Soon, what appeared to be a sedan arrived across the way, parking in the main party spot. The engine went silent, the headlights shut off. Somebody got out, the shadow dim and barely visible, but definitely there. Bobby's breath was shallow as he strained to hear voices. Then there was no movement, no noise, nothing for a long time.

Bobby worried the person wouldn't leave before daybreak, when his truck would be noticed. He surmised this person might be hostile, even dangerous—the killer—Officer Tom Wicky—returning to the scene of the crime. This terrified Bobby. He was alone with no weapon. Then he calmed down, telling himself it was probably a husband riding out here after a late-night fight with the wife. Or perhaps simply a night owl, a person who liked solitude. It could be anyone.

Finally, at four-forty, the shadow moved, the car door opened again and closed. The motor started and the headlights flashed on. Bobby prayed the car's beams would not turn his way, and by some strange grace, they didn't. But as the vehicle disappeared down the trail, suddenly, quickly, as if it were a mistake, the swing of red and blue lights spun atop the car for a second, and then faded out.

At daybreak, Bobby walked along the shore, this time further than he'd gone before, staring intensely out into the water, searching. He spent a good four hours walking around, returning home exhausted, skipping his daily workout and ignoring Penny's call. That night, after his work shift, he went home, but awoke at dawn and drove out to Baskro. Later, once more, he skipped the gym and ignored Penny's call again. On the third morning of this routine, at six a.m., he saw the lump in the distance, washed up on the shore. Bobby's heart pounded but he continued walking. It took a long while to reach it because the lump was around the far side of the lake. As he grew closer, he saw that it was probably Janine—her long black hair glistened in the morning sun, looking like a selchie, wet from the lapping of the lake's waves. Two black crows stood upon her, their heads dipped, their beaks stabbing at her body. When he drew closer, the birds hesitated before flying off, cawing with irritation. At his arrival, Bobby saw that Janine was face down, naked from the waist up, distorted, her skin greenish-black, bloated and foul, two angel tattoos barely visible on her swollen back and thick sliver rings embedded in her wrinkled blackened fingers. Parts of her skin had slipped off, revealing raw whitish flesh. Bobby was not shocked by death, but he was shaken by the distortion death and the water had done to her. He studied Janine for a long time before he realized underneath her black hair, at the right temple, there was a small black hole. A bullet hole.

He pulled out his cell and called the cops. Two young officers arrived and saw the bullet hole. They questioned Bobby, and later, a detective spoke with him some more, but it was all routine, as he was never really a suspect.

A week later, at Janine's wake, her son, a tall teenager, stood with Pete Finn in front of the closed casket. The boy's name was Stewart and he thanked Bobby for finding his mother. "Uncle Pete told me he'd asked you to help, that you'd find my mom."

Bobby didn't know what to say, so he offered his condolences.

Later, as Bobby was leaving, Finn caught up and walked him to his car. "Thanks, man," Finn said. "I knew you'd come through. I knew you'd think it was Wicky, too."

Charges were pending against Wicky, the story sensational enough to make the New York City news. Wicky had been having an affair with Janine, and, according to his confession, she'd threatened to tell his wife. He'd lost his temper and shot her, and then tossed her body in Baskro Lake.

"It was nothing, Finn," Bobby said. "It was you who knew it all along. I just followed your lead."

Finn nodded and lit a cigarette, his thick fingers shaking. "I know she was no prize, but she was my sister, you know?"

Bobby said he understood. He got in his truck and drove away.

At the gym, Moronhead pestered Bobby about a new protein shake, a blonde on a treadmill, and finally, about the death of Janine. "Do you believe a cop shot her? Fucked up shit, I tell ya."

"Yeah," Bobby muttered.

Later, he bought milk for his protein shake and sliced turkey for an afternoon sandwich at the convenience store. Finn was nowhere to be seen and for some reason, this saddened Bobby because it seemed unfair.

When he reached his house, he found Penny parked in front of it. He'd been ignoring her phone calls for a couple of weeks.

She got out, tears streaming down her face. "What's wrong, Bobby? What's going on?"

At the sight of her despair, his heart softened and he led her inside. But the sex was mediocre at best, desire lacking on his part. He realized now that he was going to drop her. He still loved Penny, but he understood that he didn't like her, didn't like that he was someone she'd never leave her husband for.

As he lay in his bed, Penny asleep beside him, Bobby thought of Janine. Wicky had probably said something similar: *You know I can't leave my wife.* Janine was tougher than most people, she had more spit in her words, more passion in her actions—so her hurt must have turned into rage, not defeat, and her blackmail must have infuriated Wicky. Even though Janine and Bobby had never meshed romantically, deep down, they were from the same pot—Janine, Finn, Bobby. And people like Wicky and Penny weren't. People like Penny and Wicky get to have the house, the two kids, the dog—hell, they get to be married and have affairs when they were unhappy—and people like Janine, people like Bobby, well, they just didn't.

Previously published in Needle: A Magazine of Noir.

ANGELS

The call comes in at nine-fifty-seven. "Sexual Assault. Pine Hollow." Followed by a couple of details. Young woman, twenty years old, injured. A fourteen-year-old boy phoned it in on his cell. He's with her now, standing on Woodland Street.

I'm not proud of this—I hesitate for five or six seconds. I've been doing this job for almost two decades and I've had my share of these calls, but usually there's too much gray, there's alcohol involved, there are accusations that may not be true. I don't mean to sound cold, I'm a woman myself, and I once had a friend who was attacked by some drugged-up frat boy, but—and I'm not saying anything nothing new here—a rape case is hard to prove. Simple, infuriating, but true.

Because I'm in the neighborhood, I'm there in one minute. I'm the first officer on the scene so I put the spotlight on. She's standing near the curb, wearing shorts and a T-shirt, her long hair hanging down, messy, her feet in socks but no shoes, both of her hands clasped desperately around a gangly young teenager's arm as if he were the last buoy in the ocean.

I step out of my cruiser and approach them.

She's hysterical, crying, mumbling about angels. The boy's eyes are wide, frightened, relieved I'm there.

"I'm Officer Andrea Vogel," I tell them.

"I was walking," the young woman blurts. "Just walking. Exercise, you know? And a guy tackled me. I don't know where he came from. I mean, I heard footsteps and I turned around and I thought it was like someone joking. But then the guy tackled me and dragged me there." She points behind her, into the darkness of the trees.

"Okay, take a breath," I tell her. "What is your name?"

"Katie Marino."

"Where did he go?"

"He ran into the woods," she says, letting her grip on the boy loosen.

"When was that?"

"I'm not sure."

The boy answers. "About ten minutes ago."

I ask if either of them recognized the perpetrator.

"No," she says, sniffling. "No."

The boy shakes his head. "I just saw a shadow."

Katie gives me a description: a man about her age, white, large, tall, muscular, wearing a royal blue T-shirt and dark shorts. I call it in immediately, relaying the possible direction of the suspect and time frame. Afterwards, I ask Katie if she lives in the neighborhood.

"Yes."

"What is your address?"

She suddenly slips into a strange reverie, blinking her eyes slowly before answering. "Five-eighty-nine."

"Five-eighty-nine what, Katie?" I keep my voice gentle.

"No," she says, shaking her head. "I mean, three-forty-eight. Five-eighty-nine is my cell number. The beginning. I'm so confused. I'm sorry."

"It's okay. We'll get the address later." I look at the boy. "What's your name?"

"Jacob Wortreich."

"What did you see?"

"I was walking and she came out of the woods screaming."

"My cell phone is gone," Katie interrupts. "I had a cell phone and he threw it."

"We'll find it," I say before turning back to Jacob. "So you didn't see the guy?"

"No, not really," he stammers. "I mean, I saw a shadow and he took off."

"Where were you going?" I ask him.

Jacob shrugs. "Nowhere. Just looking for people to hang out with, I guess."

The answer makes sense: it's Friday night, early Fall, the kid is a bit unkempt—the hair needs a cut, the sneakers are worn, the dark T-shirt has a tear at the bottom. Home rules are lax, I'm guessing.

Three cars arrive and the officers get out. I report to my colleagues, reiterate that the suspect is at large. They quickly organize a plan and begin searching the woods.

"Where are your shoes?" I ask Katie.

She begins to cry. "I took them off."

This strikes me as strange. "Why?"

She looks down. "Can I tell you later?"

More cops show up, more lights. The area is now brightly lit. I gently walk Katie to the curb, away from Jacob. She limps, moves slowly, wincing and whimpering. I help her sit down.

"I need to go to church," she says, sniffling. "I don't go, ever. Not anymore. It's terrible. I went to Catholic school all my life and I never go to church."

If the suspect is local, which I'm betting he is, this is why she didn't recognize him. Catholic school kids rarely mix with public school kids, even if they grow up in the same neighborhood. They keep to themselves. Or, at least, that's how it was when I was growing up.

"Is there someone I can call?" I ask, kneeling before her.

The young woman begins to sob. "My mom is going to be so angry. She doesn't like me walking at night."

"Do you know your mom's number?"

"No. It's in my cell phone. But he threw it." Katie wipes her nose and shifts, cringes in pain. "My legs hurt," she whispers, touching the back of her left thigh. I'm trying to keep myself composed, professional, but it's hard. She seems like a sweet kid and if I had a daughter, this would rip my heart out.

"I should know my mother's cell number," Katie says. "But she just got a new number and I can't remember it. I'm such a shitty daughter. She's not home now. She's working. At ShopRite."

"It's okay," I say. "Just give me her name."

"I don't want her to know." Katie begins to weep.

I let her cry and I stand up, relieving my legs from kneeling. At forty-six, my body isn't as limber as it once was.

"My mom," she weeps. "She's gonna be so upset."

The noise of the scene batters my ears: police radios, male voices, sirens in the distance. I crick my neck and stare into the forest which is lit up with spotlights. Trees sway in a gentle breeze. The strong scent of scrub pines permeates the air. A wide trail opens before me like the mouth of a tunnel. Yes, this guy is either from or familiar with the neighborhood. We're on the edge of the Pine Barrens, a rural area of New Jersey, in the back section of a development of houses built in the 1970s, not a place for someone who doesn't know his way around. He attacked on foot. Opportunistic crime. He's probably a loser, dropped out of community college, maybe even high school. I bet he has no car, no prospects, just trolling the dark streets, looking for something to do.

My gaze falls back to Katie and I stare at her feet. "What happened to your shoes?"

She looks up. "I took them off."

"Why?"

"Because."

I bend down again. "Because why?" I ask softly.

I can see her swallow. "Because. Because when he was, you know…" she stops talking, that same eerie gaze falling over her face. "My shorts and underwear were down, like halfway down my legs." The pace in her voice picks up and turns apologetic. "I didn't know what to do. He was really strong and his hand was around my neck. I had no choice but to let him do what he wanted."

"I know. Take a breath."

She does.

"Okay, so you tried to fight?" I ask.

"No, once he tackled me, my legs went out. I'm not strong."

"Right."

"So I let him, you know, have sex with me, but I didn't say he could. I mean, I just let it happen. I pushed my shorts and underwear around my ankles but I couldn't get them off." She shakes her head and wipes strands of hair from her face. "No, wait. I got the shorts off but my underwear was stuck. So I kicked off my sneakers and got my underwear off with my feet. I didn't want them tangled around my ankles. That way when he finished, you know, got up, I could get away and run."

I'm surprised. It's very smart.

"I don't know why I thought I could run. My legs are Jell-O. The muscles are pulled."

"Adrenaline will take you far, even with an injury."

Katie stares at me. "I think he was gonna choke me to death. I don't know. But he could have, right?"

"Yes," I tell her.

"That's why I didn't fight. I said, 'Do what you want.' I just let it happen. That's why I took my underwear off. So I could run. It wasn't because I was okay with him having sex with me. He raped me, right?"

I nod. This isn't proven yet, but if it happened the way she said it did, it's a rape.

"I didn't say it was okay," she says.

"I believe you. It sounds like you assessed the situation and did what you had to do to survive."

"I guess. I asked him if he played football because he was big, like a football player. But he told me to shut-up."

I'm completely taken aback that she tried to converse with the suspect. "When did you talk to him?"

It takes a minute but she eventually answers in a shamed whisper. "When he was on top of me."

I can feel my heart ache. "What else did you say?"

"I told him I was in college and I was studying to be a nurse. I told him if I died, my mom would be devastated. I asked him if he had a family but he told me to shut up. I told him I had a dog named Riley. I asked him if he had a dog and he said he did. I asked him what his dog's name was and he told me if I didn't stop talking, he would kill me."

I'm very impressed with her. "You made yourself a person instead of an object. That's smart, Katie."

"Yeah, I guess. I read it in a magazine."

"What magazine?"

"I don't know. *Cosmo*, I think."

"*Cosmo.*" I used to read those magazines when I was young.

"You're supposed to fight first but if you can't, you gotta use your brain."

"You did that."

"That's all I had left."

I don't know what to say. I glance at the trees as they sway in the soft wind.

"The angels were coming for me," she says.

I look at her.

Katie brushes the hair from her face again. "You can't see them. They're just floating down, coming." She begins to cry. "I didn't want them to come for me. I'm only twenty. I didn't want them to take me away."

I feel my blood stop moving.

She's quiet for a moment before speaking again. "They were coming for me so I knew that I was gonna die. I only lived because that boy walked up on us."

How odd. He said that she came out of the woods screaming. "He walked up on you?"

"Yes. He said, 'Whoa,' and the guy ran away."

"So you were on the ground?"

"Yeah. I mean, no. The guy made me stand up after you know...Anyway, he had his hand on my neck. I know I said I was gonna run but he was so strong. I just couldn't get away. And he was dragging me into the woods, like farther. And I think that's when he was gonna kill me. Like he was thinking he had to hide my body or something. That kid was walking by and I guess because I had no clothes on the bottom part of my body he was freaked out."

I don't understand why Jacob lied earlier, unless he was confused himself.

"So the guy took off and I found my underwear and shorts and put them on and I was screaming, telling the kid not to leave me because I was just raped. So he stayed with me and walked me to the street and called the police with his phone."

I look back and see Jacob standing by another police car.

"The angels were coming," she says, weeping again. "They were coming for me. That kid saved me. I need to go back to church."

ANGELS

***

They take Katie away, to the hospital for a rape kit and the morning-after pill (if she accepts, which I hope she will) and then for questioning. I report to Alan Brendler, our lead detective, that the kid lied, that the suspect has a dog. Alan raises an eyebrow and I explain about Katie's attempt to speak with the guy. "Smart girl," he says. I return to my car. It's out of my hands now. I'm not an investigator. Still, I'm part of the search which includes the entire neighborhood and beyond. Nothing turns up. I inquire about Jacob, if they got the truth out of him, but there's no information yet. Eventually my shift ends and I go home, sit at my kitchen table and drink a glass of orange juice as the sun comes up.

I have trouble sleeping so when this happens, I like to watch television. I'm a big fan of period films and shows like *Circle of Friends, Call the Midwife,* that type of thing. I can usually find something on NetFlix and I decide on *Sense and Sensibility.* My husband used to make fun of me but they bring me peace.

I can't focus, though. Katie's angels haunt me and I lay in bed, staring at the TV, thinking about them. Even though she said they couldn't be seen, I keep picturing gliding objects, sailing down from the trees. Only my angels are shadows, dark, like large bats in slow motion. Soon I'm thinking about

Marie, about that night she called, begging me to come down to her dorm room. I found her alone, her roommate gone for the weekend. As soon as I shut the door, she started blubbering, throwing out bits and pieces of the night. She was drinking and so was he, but he was on something else, coke, she thought. They were just kissing, that she'd met him after I'd left the party. They went back to his place. When she told him she didn't want to do anything he threw her on the bed, overpowering her. "I couldn't fight him off." I insisted she call the police but Marie protested, explaining that everyone knows that when you're drinking, they can't prove anything, so don't bother. I told her she looked a mess, that she looked like she was raped, that they'd definitely believe her. Finally, at four a.m., I talked her into going to the police station. She was reeking of alcohol but she seemed sober enough tell her story. Nothing came of it. In fact, Marie blamed me for embarrassing her by making her go.

I turn over in bed. My dead husband comes to mind and I suddenly remember what he said, years later, after I'd told him the story of Marie. "I'm sure the guy didn't realize what he was doing," Carl said. "She was drinking and he was drinking and doing drugs. Maybe he thought she was okay with it all."

"She told him to stop."

"She was drunk, Andie. She probably *thought* she told him to stop."

I loved my husband and Lord knows I miss him terribly. He was a good man, kind, faithful. But now I remember something I had forgotten: I remember how I recoiled at his response, how his words settled in my bones, like a dark oil that wouldn't wash away for weeks.

Sunday afternoon, Alan sends me to Katie's house to take pictures. Mrs. Marino had phoned in the morning and reported that Katie's legs were extremely bruised, as was her neck. I dread telling Katie and her mother that the guy hasn't been caught yet.

Katie is subdued, spacey almost, barely talks. She turns around and hesitantly lifts her shorts halfway over her buttocks. Dark ugly bruises have bloomed there and on the back of her thighs, the bend in her legs. Hamstring damage from being violently tackled to the ground. The sight is shocking but I keep composed. I snap the pictures, assuring her she's doing well. I ask her to face me and push her hair back so I can take photos of her neck. The bruises aren't as severe—grayish purple and yellow—but the spots are telling: one on the left, four on the right. All from his fingers. Evidence she was choked.

When we are done, Katie nods, mutters "thank you," and limps down the hallway into her bedroom. The difference in Katie's demeanor is jarring: the terrified but talkative, smart girl from Saturday night is now broken: shoulders slumped, quiet, crippled with shame. Rape victims have the most trouble with this—the shame.

Katie's mother appears from the kitchen, followed by a large Golden Retriever. Riley. Both had left the room earlier when I'd pulled out the camera.

"You haven't found him yet?" Katie's mother asks. Her arms are crossed over her chest.

"No, Mrs. Marino."

"No leads?"

"The detectives have high priority on this."

"Bullshit."

I frown.

"So you know it's bullshit?" she says.

"I didn't say that."

"But you know it."

"Trust me," I say. "They're looking." Extra patrols have been put out. Police from neighboring towns are on alert.

Mrs. Marino points at me. "I told Katie this was gonna happen. I told her she can't go walking at night. It's not smart, right?"

I don't want to lie. "It puts a woman at risk."

Mrs. Marino huffs, swallows, bites her lip. Her eyes grow wet. "Katie won't talk to me. She just sits in her room, listening to her iPod."

Riley leans his head against Mrs. Marino.

"Give her time," I say.

"She's scared. She thinks he's going to come back."

I say nothing. It's a legitimate fear.

Katie's mother wipes the tears from her eyes. "I don't think I could have lived if he killed her."

"But she survived."

"I know. That's the most important thing. I keep telling myself this."

Mrs. Marino's sorrow burrows under my skin as I drive back to the station. Soon I think of Jacob. I know I'm not one of the investigators on the case and I know they grilled the kid, but there's something there. He knows something. Yes, he admitted that he had lied to me about Katie coming out of the woods screaming, but he told Alan Brendler and the other detective that he didn't mean to, that his head was a little messed up. It's believable. Innocent people make mistakes when they recall a crime. Still, this kid isn't being completely forthright.

When I arrive at the station, I ask Alan if he got any headway with the boy.

"He said he didn't recognize the guy."

"Did you have him take a wild guess?"

"Yes, we did, Andie. He had nothing."

It still sits unevenly. "Something's off," I say. "Everyone knows everyone in that neighborhood." I take a seat in front of Alan's desk and study the bonsai plant on the shelf. My thoughts turn over and over. Kids notice things. I remember when I was young, when I rode my bike through the streets of my development, I knew who lived where, what they looked like, even some of their habits. My friends and I even rode our bikes at night and because we lived in walking distance to a convenience store and a beer and shot bar, even in the dark we could tell who was who just by their amble. I bet Jacob has a good guess.

"Can I talk to him?"

Alan leans back in his chair. "I don't know, Andie. The kid was pretty spooked by the entire situation. He didn't see the guy."

It's a load of crap. Maybe I'm just head-strong, stubborn, as Carl used to say, but sometimes you have to be. "Let me have a word with him."

The detective puts his hands behind his head. "Give it a shot."

Jacob is on the corner of his street, shooting hoops, while a group of kids sit nearby. It's a motley-looking crew: three boys and a girl, early teens, all perched on the curb, one of them is smoking, the others are drinking from soda bottles. Jacob stares at me when I get out of the cruiser. The kids straighten up as I approach. The one boy places the cigarette on the ground and covers it with his sneaker.

"Hello, Officer," the girl says when I arrive.

"We're just hanging," another boy adds.

I ignore them and address Jacob. "I would like to speak with you."

Reluctantly, he tucks the basketball under his arm and steps towards me. He's so young. His forehead is dotted in red pimples. He's wearing a black Nike T-shirt and green shorts, the same worn sneakers from the other night, and his short hair is still a bit overgrown. His friends get up, chuckle, mumble "better you than me," and make their way down the street. The girl turns and grins, and they all break out into a fit of laughter.

"You can keep shooting, if you want," I tell Jacob.

He bounces the ball but doesn't say anything, doesn't make eye contact.

"You did a good thing, calling the police the other night. That was very brave."

"Not really," he mutters.

"Yes, really. A lot of kids would have run away from a screaming woman. A lot of kids would have taken off if they encountered a large man who had just hurt someone. But you stayed and called the police. You didn't care if the guy came after you."

"He ran into the woods. I wasn't scared he was gonna come back."

I don't believe him. "Yes, you were."

Jacob looks up at me. His eyes are golden brown. "Maybe I was scared a little."

"You gave us good information."

He shrugs.

I gesture to his friends down the street. "You know a lot of people around here?"

"Yeah."

"I did, too, when I was a kid in my neighborhood."

"I've lived here my whole life," he remarks.

I smile at him. "It's not so bad."

"It sucks. Nothing to do."

"Yeah, I used to think the same way."

He bounces the ball.

"Did you tell your friends what happened the other night?"

"No," Jacob says quietly. "I mean, everyone knows something bad happened but nobody knows I was there."

"That's good," I say.

"Yeah," he mutters and twirls the ball in his hands.

"If you were to take a guess, just a wild, crazy guess, who would you say was that guy the other night?"

"I don't know."

"Just a guess."

Jacob bounces the ball twice. Then shrugs.

"I know it was dark but you saw his body," I say. "You probably noticed a gesture, a little thing that he did, or maybe his posture, the way he moved and you may have thought, 'Hey, that's so-and-so.' But it probably flew out of your head because rapists aren't supposed to be guys you know, right?"

"Yeah."

"So go back to that moment, when you walked up on the scene. What flew in your head and flew right out?"

"Nothing." He bounces the ball a few more times and I don't say anything.

"I don't know," Jacob mutters.

"You were brave. I need you to be brave enough to finish the job."

Jacob puts the ball on the ground and places his foot over it. He stares down the quiet street. His friends have disappeared.

"What name flew in your head?" I ask.

Jacob rubs his eye.

"You know it," I say, my voice growing firm.

The kid takes his foot off the basketball and lets it roll to the side.

"Go ahead," I push.

Jacob looks at me. "Tim Jeffers."

I nod.

"But I can't say for sure."

"Of course not."

"Don't tell anyone I said it, okay?"

"I won't." DNA was taken during the rape kit. When he's located, they'll test him.

"He doesn't live in this neighborhood," Jacob explains. "But he doesn't live far. He was a friend of my brother's. A long time ago. I haven't seen him in a couple of years because my brother says he's an asshole."

I nod again.

"But I'm not sure. I didn't see his face. It was just his size and the way he turned or something. And it was just like you said—his name flew in my head and flew out. I didn't want to tell the other cops that because I wasn't sure. And I'm not a snitch. But that lady was pretty hurt and upset." Jacob pauses for a moment and then looks at me. "It isn't right to accuse a person if you're not one hundred percent sure."

"Your brother told you that?"

"Yeah."

"Your brother also told you Tim Jeffers is an a-hole."

"Yeah, but that doesn't mean I want him to go to jail for something he didn't do."

"I understand." I hear a dog bark in the distance. "We don't send people to jail unless we have one hundred percent proof."

"So you'll just like, question him?"

"Yes. And if it comes out that he didn't do it, then he'll go on his merry way." The word *merry* leaves a tinny taste in my mouth.

Jacob nods. "So you'll test his DNA?"

I smile gently at him. "Yes."

"Okay," Jacob says. "That's good."

"Yes."

"And you won't tell anyone that I told you?"

I'm not comfortable lying to him. But I do anyway. "It will be like an anonymous tip."

Jacob beams, proud. "Cool."

The DNA matches. Timothy Jeffers, twenty-two, six-foot-one, two hundred and twenty pounds of muscle, denies it was a rape. "She said it was okay. She even took off her clothes."

He has no money so a public defender is appointed, a thin guy who advises Tim to confess. It takes three weeks before he admits that his intention was to rape Katie. That there was no consensual sex, that he overpowered her, that he choked her until she said, "Do what you want."

Four months after the attack, long after the autumn has come and gone, after the Christmas lights are taken down in the neighborhoods, after the first snowfall, Katie takes the stand in the sentencing. She wants to make sure Timothy Jeffers gets the maximum amount for the rape and the best way to do that is to appear before the judge and tell her story. I take a seat in the back of the courtroom, near Timothy's mother. She sits with her pocket book on her lap, her hands gripped on the handles. She's older, worn, sad, a woman who looks like she worked a shit job most of her life. There's a pang of melancholy that hits me in the heart. How it must hurt to be the mother of a rapist.

I listen to Katie, who speaks quietly, recalling the events of that awful night. I see Timothy Jeffers sitting with several other prisoners, all dressed in orange jumpsuits, listening to her talk about kicking off her sneakers and pulling off her underwear. I glance at Timothy's mother and notice she doesn't cry, doesn't takes out a tissue, just remains stone-still, her hands gripped on the purse's handles. When the judge hands down fifteen years, I watch Mrs. Marino place her arm around her daughter and there's a soft cry from Katie.

Later, I see Katie and her mother in the lobby. I don't approach them, just nod my head. Mrs. Marino smiles but Katie looks the other way. She appears tired, in need of a good night's sleep.

I head home, depressed. I change out of uniform, drive to the next town and buy a six-pack, wondering about Katie's angels. I'm not religious but Katie, her angels and her manic voice, the sobbing, the sniffling, her feral soul that night—it all runs wild in my mind. Those angels. *I didn't want them to come for me...*

Later, as I sit at my kitchen table drinking a beer, I tell myself that the angels were just adrenaline, a chemical in our brains that forces us to survive, to think clearly. I finish my beer and open another one.

Or maybe the angels were coming down to help

her survive. This sits with me for a while.

I can't say that I'm not bothered that Katie Marino didn't acknowledge me. That she barely said a word when I took the photos or that she wouldn't look at me in the lobby of the courthouse. But this is how it goes. When you're raped, you want to delete everything and everyone that is tied to the crime. At least for a while.

A few years ago, Marie sent me a card—an apology letter. She lives in Vermont now. The letter said she was sorry for getting angry with me. That throughout the years, she had questioned herself, whether it had been a rape or simply a bad night.

I lean back in the chair. Stare. I should read the letter again.

I get up and take another beer out of the refrigerator. The card is tucked away in a plastic tote in the spare bedroom. It takes about ten minutes, but I find it. I jump to this part:

And even if my head mixes it up, which it still does, I remember you were there and you were driving me to the police station and I remember that you believed me. That you tried to help. I'm sorry if I didn't thank you. I'm sorry that I ignored you after that. Maybe I was so ashamed it was too hard to be friends. But you have to know, the fact that you tried to help comforts me now and reminds me that it did happen, that I'm not crazy.

I know Katie Marino has a long road of grief ahead of her. I'm sure something dies in a person when they're forced to have sex. It's such an intimate, humiliating crime. Hopefully, as time goes by, Katie will think of Jacob and she'll think of me. Maybe it will make the memory just a bit easier.

I get a fourth and last beer and turn on the television. They're running *Downton Abbey* on PBS and soon I'm swept away into this far-off, imaginary world.

Previously published in Needle: A Magazine of Noir.

ACKNOWLEDGMENTS

Thank you to the great Karen Heuler for taking me under your wing and pushing me to write better and stronger. Your guidance and help has been a godsend. Thank you to my writing group: Gail Conboy, Yume Kitasei, Alix Charles, Alan Cafferkey, and the many others who came through our NYC group and offered critiques, advice, and suggestions.

Many thanks to all the editors who published my stories over the years. It's been an honor to have my work in your super cool publications.

Thanks to my son, my dad, and my sister for your support and to my fiancé, Jason, who will sit with me for hours and help me iron out a plot.

Thank you to my mom, Mary Seiderer Taylor, who passed in 2008 and always loved a good story. Wish you were here.

Jen Conley's short stories have appeared in
*Thuglit, Needle: A Magazine of Noir, Crime
Factory, Beat to a Pulp, Out of the Gutter,
Trouble in the Heartland: Crime Fiction Inspired
by the Songs of Bruce Springsteen* and many
others. She has contributed to the *Los Angeles
Review of Books* and is one of editors of *Shotgun
Honey*. She lives in New Jersey.

Twitter: @jenconley45

OTHER TITLES FROM DOWN AND OUT BOOKS

See www.DownAndOutBooks.com for complete list

By J.L. Abramo
Catching Water in a Net
Clutching at Straws
Counting to Infinity
Gravesend
Chasing Charlie Chan
Circling the Runway
Brooklyn Justice

By Trey R. Barker
2,000 Miles to Open Road
Road Gig: A Novella
Exit Blood
Death is Not Forever
No Harder Prison

By Richard Barre
The Innocents
Bearing Secrets
Christmas Stories
The Ghosts of Morning
Blackheart Highway
Burning Moon
Echo Bay
Lost

By Eric Beetner and
JB Kohl
Over Their Heads

By Eric Beetner and
Frank Scalise
The Backlist
The Shortlist (*)

By G.J. Brown
Falling

By Rob Brunet
Stinking Rich

By Mark Coggins
No Hard Feelings

By Tom Crowley
Vipers Tail
Murder in the Slaughterhouse

By Frank De Blase
Pine Box for a Pin-Up
Busted Valentines and Other
Dark Delights
A Cougar's Kiss (*)

By Les Edgerton
The Genuine, Imitation, Plastic
Kidnapping

By A.C. Frieden
Tranquility Denied
The Serpent's Game
The Pyongyang Option (*)

By Jack Getze
Big Numbers
Big Money
Big Mojo
Big Shoes

(*)—Coming Soon

OTHER TITLES FROM DOWN AND OUT BOOKS

See www.DownAndOutBooks.com for complete list

By Richard Godwin
Wrong Crowd
Buffalo and Sour Mash (*)

By Jeffery Hess
Beachhead

By Matt Hilton
No Going Back
Rules of Honor
The Lawless Kind
The Devil's Anvil

By David Housewright
Finders Keepers
Full House

By Jerry Kennealy
Screen Test (*)

By S.W. Lauden
Crosswise

By Terrence McCauley
The Devil Dogs of Belleau Wood

By Bill Moody
Czechmate
The Man in Red Square
Solo Hand
The Death of a Tenor Man
The Sound of the Trumpet
Bird Lives!

By Gary Phillips
The Perpetrators
Scoundrels (Editor)
Treacherous
3 the Hard Way

By Tom Pitts
Hustle (*)

By Robert J. Randisi
Upon My Soul
Souls of the Dead
Envy the Dead (*)

By Ryan Sayles
The Subtle Art of Brutality
Warpath
Swansongs Always Begin as Love Songs (*)

By John Shepphird
The Shill
Kill the Shill
Beware the Shill (*)

By Ian Thurman
Grand Trunk and Shearer (*)

By Lono Waiwaiole
Wiley's Lament
Wiley's Shuffle
Wiley's Refrain
Dark Paradise

(*)—Coming Soon